NORTH OF FORSAKEN

A ROAMER WESTERN

North of Forsaken

Matthew P. Mayo

FIVE STAR

A part of Gale, Cengage Learning

GALE
CENGAGE Learning

Farmington Hills, Mich • San Francisco • New York • Waterville, Maine
Meriden, Conn • Mason, Ohio • Chicago

GALE
CENGAGE Learning®

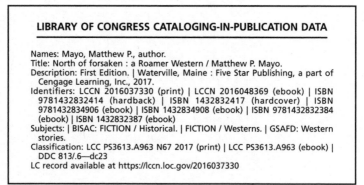

LIBRARY OF CONGRESS CATALOGING-IN-PUBLICATION DATA

Names: Mayo, Matthew P., author.
Title: North of forsaken : a Roamer Western / Matthew P. Mayo.
Description: First Edition. | Waterville, Maine : Five Star Publishing, a part of Cengage Learning, Inc., 2017.
Identifiers: LCCN 2016037330 (print) | LCCN 2016048369 (ebook) | ISBN 9781432832414 (hardback) | ISBN 1432832417 (hardcover) | ISBN 9781432834906 (ebook) | ISBN 1432834908 (ebook) | ISBN 9781432832384 (ebook) | ISBN 1432832387 (ebook)
Subjects: | BISAC: FICTION / Historical. | FICTION / Westerns. | GSAFD: Western stories.
Classification: LCC PS3613.A963 N67 2017 (print) | LCC PS3613.A963 (ebook) | DDC 813/.6—dc23
LC record available at https://lccn.loc.gov/2016037330

First Edition. First Printing: January 2017
Find us on Facebook— https://www.facebook.com/FiveStarCengage
Visit our website— http://www.gale.cengage.com/fivestar/
Contact Five Star™ Publishing at FiveStar@cengage.com

Printed in the United States of America
1 2 3 4 5 6 7 21 20 19 18 17

To Mean Pete and Miss Syd,
who know the true worth of a darn good sidekick.

"The antidote for fifty enemies is one friend."

—Aristotle

CHAPTER ONE

The rank tang of shit-stomped mud hung heavy in the dead autumn air. The street was busy, it being market day in the grubby little flyblown town of Forsaken, Wyoming. Never was a place more aptly named. I took in the dark storefronts, the clots of people moving not with intent but with the slow steps of resignation. Life on the frontier is difficult, to be sure, and it's even tougher on some than others. From the looks of this town, hardship and deprivation were two of the more familiar traits the fine folks of Forsaken had to contend with.

"Scorfano? Scorfano!"

I walked a few steps before I realized the shouting voice was hailing me. Indeed, the word being shouted was my given name at birth. Scorfano means *ugly one* in Italian. The second cruel trick my father played on me—saddling me with that maligning name. The first was fathering me at all. Apt though it may be, it is not a name I like. And the only people who once knew me by that name would not know me now.

I had left them all behind, back East, on the eve of my thirteenth birthday, though I was nearly a grown man by that time—at least in stature. I hadn't heard that name in fifteen years. I'd spent that time doing my best to grow up in other ways. And trying to lose myself in the West. Mostly it hasn't worked.

A sudden gust of windblown grit pelted my face. I sighed and turned to see who was calling to me. I should have kept on walking. Hell, I should have run.

"It is you!"

A young man in bright blue dandy garb walked toward me. His clothes warred with the drab, earthy tones surrounding him as he crossed the street and walked straight into the path of an oncoming team of draft animals. The farmer driving them yarned hard on the reins, halting the mammoth beasts in time to avoid killing the young fool, who barely gave the situation a glance. He merely tossed the red-faced farmer a wave of forgiveness.

The young man smiled as he advanced on me. He didn't see the farmer leap down from his wagon seat and in two strides reach him. The beefy man of the fields balled the velvet lapels of the young man's fancy-cut frock coat.

"See . . . see here!" sputtered the young man. "Do you know who I am?"

"Don't care," spat the farmer through gritted teeth, "but you'll soon be less toothy." The farmer's Teutonic accent was as angular as his ropy forearms were thick. And he pulled one of those arms back for a straight-on ramming at the young fool's as-yet-unmarred countenance.

I don't normally interfere in other men's quarrels—it's a good way to wind up hurt or worse—but technically I was the cause of this dispute, though I knew not why.

I stepped in quick, and though the farmer himself was a brute of a man, every inch and then some of six feet, and as wide as a wagon wheel, I am rarely overpowered in height and girth. I am on the north end of six foot four and carry little in the way of paunch, or what my good friend, Maple Jack, refers to as "reserve flesh for hard times." My hand closed around the farmer's wrist and held fast, stalling the vicious blow, and he turned a bright red face from the young man to me.

An oath of anger died on the farmer's lips as his wide eyes

took in my facial features. As I mentioned, I am not a pretty man. Truth be told, I am one of the homelier men you are ever likely to meet—a top lip split from birth beneath spiky black whiskers, pocked cheeks, an oft-broken nose, and dark eyes set in a wide, blocky head. What cruel quirks of circumstance conspired to make me so aberrant, I know not, nor do I care at this point. What's done is done.

"Friend," I said, smiling through my beard stubble. "The greenhorn meant no harm. And besides, he is no match for you." I straightened and looked down at the farmer, letting my unspoken invitation settle on him like street dust on new shoes. The spark of rage in his eyes dimmed. As I released his wrist he yanked, to show he could maintain a head of steam. I let him. His other hand freed the greenhorn with a shove and a flick from his meaty fingertips, as if he were shooing a bluebottle fly.

Only then did I see that the entire town had paused in its duties, every eye of its meager populace fixed on the scene, pleading, hungering for excitement . . . for blood. As the German farmer strode to his wagon, I saw outright disappointment on not a few of the staring faces. Within seconds a small swarm of the farmer's cronies clustered about him, yammering as groups of men will do—as much or more so than any clutch of women—cutting their eyes now and again in my direction.

"Thank you. I—"

I had momentarily forgotten about the fool who caused this ruckus, who I had not yet looked upon at this close range.

I faced him and got a good look at the young man then. Of course up close I knew him. His was a face I doubted I'd ever see again in all my days.

Unruffled by the recent affront to his dignity, the young man smoothed his lapels and smiled up at me, stretching his neck forward. "It is you, Scorfano! I never thought to see you again and certainly never expected to find you of all people here in this . . . this savage wasteland!"

"Thomas," I said, nodding down at him. For in truth, I could think of nothing else to say.

He fidgeted in the street, with the entire town watching, and finally grasped me tight about the middle with both arms, his blue derby hat with a wide, black silk band falling to the rutted street. I pushed him away.

"It's so good to see you," he said, retrieving the garish topper.

I knew if I asked him anything at all, there would be nothing for it but to listen to him explain every minute of the past fifteen years. And as I recalled, he was a talker even as a child. I saw no reason why that should have changed. By my math he was but twenty-two years old, and he looked less than that age. The intervening years had been kind to him.

"I have to go," I said, turning away.

His frantic little boy's voice reached me and I felt his hand on my arm. "You can't leave like that. Old friends and all."

I kept walking toward the livery, temporary quarters for my big Percheron stallion, Tiny Boy. Thomas worked hard to keep up with me. When I've a mind, I can scissor my legs faster than any man I know and can cover a lot of ground in the process.

"Scorfano . . . wait! At least let me buy you a drink. Or perhaps a meal?"

I kept walking.

"Please," he said. "Slow down!" I heard his voice begin to take on a frantic, desperate edge I did not expect. Then in a lower tone he said, "I need help. I fear I may be in grave danger."

I closed my eyes and stopped, knowing I would come to regret this decision for a long time. I turned around.

"One drink," I said. "I have places to go."

He smiled again and I saw the same brown-headed boy I had played with so long ago, in a different life and in a different time. For a moment, I could almost believe I was looking into the eyes of a friend.

Like I said before, I should have run.

CHAPTER TWO

I led the way to the Square Deal Saloon, the only one of a half dozen such establishments in Forsaken that didn't have an assortment of drunks twitching outside the batwings. Once my eyes adjusted to the dimness of the bar, I took in the room with a quick sweep. It pays to get a bearing on your whereabouts, and adjust it as you go.

This one looked and smelled much the same as all the others I'd been in over the years—not clean, by any stretch, but sporting that worn, comfortable look only oft-frequented bars get. It was a one-story affair. The close air smelled of the musky stink of sweat, old beer, and other scents I didn't care to dwell on.

Off to the left, in the far back corner, stood a precarious stack of snapped and crippled chairs. They'd been there a while. In their place at the four card tables were arranged nail kegs, some with sacking puffed up and tacked around the edges. The floor appeared to be little more than sawdust and dried clods of mud, though here and there rough planking was visible.

The whole affair was streaked with tobacco juice like brown leavings. As if a flock of birds with gut trouble had flown through. On the trail, I like a chaw now and again, but refrain from using it in town. I'm always afraid I'll be caught whipping a stream of spit in front of a lady. I have enough trouble keeping from drawing attention to myself, I don't need to add to it.

The bar itself was a fixed structure, not planks on barrels as so many others are. Evidently Forsaken had ambitions to rise above its name. I suspect that given enough time even the name would change. Probably something more cheerful like Hope Springs. I'll ride clear of that one.

I palmed the bar, and the keep nodded at us, waiting.

"What'll you have?" I said, looking at my companion for the first time since we left the street. He smiled, swept off that silly blue derby, and placed it on the sticky bartop as if it had value. "Never trust a man in a derby or a bowler," says Maple Jack, my old trapping friend. And while I am inclined to shy away from generalizations, preferring to judge a man on his merits as I get to know him, I will say I have rarely seen Jack proved wrong in his assessment of people. I call it uncanny. He calls it a product of old age.

"Good day, my friend," said Thomas to the keep. "A dram of your finest malt all around." He swept an arm that almost clipped my chin. The four other men in the place, barkeep included, stared in our direction as if something dead had festered in the sun then crawled in to find a little shade.

"Ain't no malt in here mister. Just whiskey and beer."

Thomas nodded as if in agreement. "Whiskey, then!"

"You don't have to do that," I said in a low voice. "You don't know these people."

"Know them?" he said. "They are witness to the rebirth of an old friendship."

I didn't know what to say, but I wished I had not acknowledged his greeting on the street.

When the drinks had been passed around, the grunts of thanks offered by the other patrons, and his money paid, I waited for the inevitable questions. And he obliged me.

"So, where have you been, Scorfano? It has been, what, a dozen years since you left?" He sipped, grimaced as the tanglefoot scorched his throat, never taking his eyes from my face. "You never said where you were heading, never sent word as to your whereabouts. I missed you, Scorfano. You were like an older brother to me."

I bit back angry words, words that change situations, words that have no place but buried in the past. "I had to leave. It was time," I said. "And it's been fifteen years."

"Fifteen . . ." His face took on that long look of deep disbelief that comes to all of us when we realize we've lost hunks of our lives to the steady roll of life's clock. "Where did it go?"

I looked back to my drink. Toyed with the glass.

"They picked on me, you know," he said. "Said I wasn't to play with the stable boy."

I could tell he was looking at me for a reaction. I would not oblige him.

He continued, "I fished at the bridge a few more times after you left, but it wasn't the same. Even Mimsy stopped talking about you."

He got me with that one. The one name in all the world I hadn't allowed myself to think back on for years, had forced down to the bottom of the war bag in my mind. Mimsy. The closest I'd ever come to having a mother. A harsh woman, to be sure, but a good old woman. And the cause of the sole regret I've harbored since taking to the open trails of the West. I didn't dare ask, though by my clenched jaw muscles and the way I pressed my fingers to the bartop, Thomas no doubt guessed my question.

"Scorfano," he said in a low voice. "Scorfano, old friend, please look at me."

I sighed and half turned toward him.

"Mimsy is gone. A long time ago."

My vile features settled deeper into themselves then and I looked away from him, from the sadness and pity in his little boy's eyes. I pushed back from the bar and inhaled deeply. "Was it me?" I said, low, hoping he had not heard me.

A tall, horse-faced man in a ragged brown coat bumped my shoulder on his way to the door, mumbled something I didn't hear.

Thomas swallowed the last of his shot and nudged his glass. "She did not last a year after you left. We were all upset by this." He looked at me again. "My parents, also gone. Both of them."

That news affected me far less than hearing Mimsy had passed. Thomas's parents were my parents, nothing he ever need know. And their deaths did not bother me.

I looked him in the eye. "For your sake I am truly sorry to hear that, Thomas."

He looked as if he were about to speak once more.

"I have to go." I pushed by him. "It's been good to see you. Good luck to you."

He put a hand on my arm, looked up at me, his eyes hard and bright. "They all blamed you. All of them. Mother, Father . . . But I didn't believe it. Not for one moment. And neither did Mimsy."

He was kind, as I remembered him, but he was wrong. The parents, I could care less about. But Mimsy . . . I killed that poor old woman as surely as if I had shot her. I broke her heart. But only after she broke mine.

"Good-bye, Thomas." I pushed past him and out the door, into the sunshine-filled afternoon.

He didn't follow me, and for that I was grateful. I needed to be alone. I needed to not think about all the people in my past. As I descended one boardwalk, making for another toward the mercantile, a woman's brief, sharp shout of surprise cut the air.

"That's him!" she shouted.

I looked up to see a burly, jowl-faced woman two buildings ahead, pointing at me and scowling. She wore a flouncy, bruise-colored dress far too fancy for her squat build, and as unsuited

17

to this town as a diamond necklace would be on a javelina. A white-gloved hand fluttered at her throat like a confused pigeon.

Beside her stood a smallish, thin man in a dark jacket and gray brocade vest, knee-high boots of black leather, polished to a sheen, and a black derby perched atop his pate. Below his chin he sported a cravat matching the woman's dress. A wide sneer spread across his mouth, leaving him looking like a satisfied catfish. His whiskers looked to be a load of work, all shaped and waxed to points. His eyes, hard and dark, narrowed and glinted.

Behind him I saw a brown shape, a tall man, whose long face looked familiar, but from where I didn't recall. And then I did— the man from the bar. The one who'd looked at us longer than most when I first walked in there. The same man who'd pushed by me, knocking against me on his way to the door not five minutes before. So that was the game—send in a ringer, find out when I'd be leaving, then wait for me. Wait to set me up. But why?

I've been down this road too many times before. Nearly always, my accusers have mistaken me for someone else. And nearly always I'm at least interrogated by the marshal or a deputy eager to prove he's filling his boots in good order. This had the stink of a put-up job from the moment the woman mouthed her fake scream. And I had no intention of putting up with this one. Not today, I thought. All I wanted to do was hit the trail, visit with Maple Jack, then head deeper into the mountains.

I shook my head, barely gave them a look, and kept walking. I strode up onto their boardwalk, edged through the crowd of onlookers and past them, and the small dandy man shouted, "Someone stop him! He's wronged my wife!"

I wanted to keep walking, but I knew, especially with my back turned, that someone would ambush me. It's happened before. All for the honor of a woman who probably had none.

I turned, head tilted to one side, and looked at them as a schoolmarm might an unruly class. I rested a hand on the butt of my Schofield revolver and said, "Now look, I never saw you people in my life. All I've done in this town is have a drink and buy a few supplies. I'm on my way out of here right now."

I heard someone shout, "Liar!"

Then things happened.

For the record, I didn't swing first. I do, as a rule, try to swing last. Unfortunately that doesn't always work out the way I plan. It all depends on what you're swinging. In your average fisticuffs match, I usually fare well. My fists and my reach are more than most men's, unless they're swinging a stout stick. I've been hit enough to know what the feeling is like, but for some reason I've never been able to fathom, a man who's hit right above the ear will drop like a sack of wet sand.

And as rugged as I like to claim I am, I am no exception to the rule. Being a connoisseur of attacks and clubbings, I can usually tell what it is I'm being hit with. This time I'd have to guess it was an ax handle. The weight, the odd-shaped circumference, the solid hickory smack as the handle connected with the side of my head left little doubt that I was about to drop like that heavy wet sack I mentioned.

The familiar but unwelcome flowering of heat up the side of my head, the accompanying flash of blue-white light, like lightning over distant peaks, the sudden sticky taste of blood in my nose and throat, and always, the same thought occurs to me: How many such knocks can a man take before he goes dotty in the head? If I were a betting man, I'd lay odds I'll find out one of these days.

CHAPTER THREE

I came around in full and dark quiet. As I lay there letting my brain figure itself out, what had happened on the sidewalk in Forsaken dribbled back to me. I did my best to pretend it was a bad dream, tried like hell to convince myself I was rolled in my blankets in a clearing of my own choosing, Tiny Boy hobbled and napping out of sight of the dwindled campfire. I hoped it was the wee hours and that soon I would feel the urge to rise, take care of my business in the alders, then boil up a pot of hot coffee on the fire.

Yes, that's what I hoped for, but as Maple Jack told me long ago, "Hope in one hand, mess in the other, see which fills faster." I groped with my fingers and felt the firmness of a ticked mattress, the smooth wood edge of a well-used cot, and confirmed what I already knew, though I hadn't let my wishes in on the truth yet: I was in a cell, once again. And near as I could remember, once again it wasn't my fault. But this time it was more than my hard looks and the fears of locals that had landed me in the lockup. I had the feeling this time there was more to the story.

I was still fuzzy headed, and passed in and out of a sleeplike daze, thoughts of my childhood flooding unbidden into my mind. Thomas's appearance and subsequent news served to stir up what I had thought were long-forgotten memories. Now I know they were only sediment settled for a time at the bottom of a deep well. Who knows what else rests there?

How long I lay like that I'm not sure. Images of who I was, who I am, floated in and out of my head like characters playing parts on a stage. I heard voices, men, women, children, old and young, all chanting names I'd heard hurled my way through the years. From the Yukon to Mexico, from Virginia to California I've been called nomad, drifter, vagabond, wanderer, roamer, rover, rambler, restless spirit, no-good tramp, and a few others I can't recall. And I've earned a few of them, I'm sure. The harsher-spirited folks usually prefaced the name with the word ugly. The Blackfeet called me Ocritou, which means *ugly one*. And I've earned that, too.

On top of it all, I've been accused of being born under a bad sign. And while I'm not much for such notions, I will admit I lead a life that sees more than its fair share of hardships and low points. Wherever I go, trouble follows like a half-starved dog after a meat wagon.

I thought of Maple Jack, the trapper from New England with whom I spend much time and one of the few folks I ever formed a strong bond with. Years before he had taken to calling me Roamer in much the same way an uncle might call a nephew "youngster" or "boy." I didn't mind the name. He said it suited me, and, though, I did tell him the name I was given at birth, I preferred to be called something, anything else.

When a man's natural inclination is to be left alone, coupled with the fact that a face like mine is more closely associated with outlaws and bad men thinking bad thoughts and doing dark deeds, the suspicions of good folks are naturally aroused. From what I can tell, I lack that most basic of animal tendencies—the urge to be with others of one's kind, to be part of a community, not apart from it.

And that's the biggest reason why I am regarded with suspicion, I would say. I like my own company. I don't mind being around other folks, but I'm always relieved when it's time to part. Perhaps one day that will change. But the way I look and the way I feel—is the one responsible for the other?—I'll be regarded with suspicion for some time to come. And I guess I don't mind.

I've come close to death on a number of occasions, and for a few days following each time my thoughts will betray me and ride roughshod over the intention I have set out for myself in this life, namely to keep to myself and get lost in the wide-open West.

It seems that, despite my own stated claims, there is a part of me buried deep who yearns for that which I travel away from—family, friends, the closeness of a community, the predictability of a life lived in one place, the unparalleled companionship of siblings.

I thought of the two brothers who had robbed me a few years before. As vile as they seemed, they meant something to each other. I, on the other hand, meant something only to myself, and perhaps, also, to Maple Jack. But when had it ever been otherwise? My entire life had been lived largely in solitude. Even as a child when I was among a good many people, I was a lone figure.

In that cell I wondered how many people's lives were determined largely by news they learn in the span of two minutes. News they were not supposed to hear. The awful truth of my life was concealed from me until the night before my thirteenth birthday. I overheard Mimsy, the head cook and the woman who had raised me. She was in her cups as she was most evenings by that time, warning the newest chambermaid, Polly, to refrain from any conversation with me. She said I was a bad seed and it would only lead to her being let go from her position.

I felt as though I'd been kicked in the gut by a mule. An anger I had never before known washed over me, and to date it hasn't left me. I was seconds from bursting into the room and demanding to know why she said such harsh words. But she had continued speaking. I checked my youthful impulse and instead I listened. And it was in those next two minutes the entire course of my life altered.

I learned that night that I am eldest of two children by a woman for whom the word "mother" was as inappropriate as the word "pretty" would be in describing me. She was the daughter of a wealthy plantation owner, and she married a well-titled young Italian man with some vague military standing. From what I'd gathered through the years, he did little in the way of officering and much in the way of justifying the incredible amount of time he spent entertaining.

According to Mimsy, I was so unattractive at birth, the woman who bore the shame of having given birth to me refused me immediately. I was supposed to have been given the full family name of my father and my father's father, and so on back through the line. But I was not the child they had expected and was instead disowned, ignored as the firstborn son.

They stuck me with the name Scorfano, a cruel joke in itself, as it described my unfortunate features and none of my lineage. Their only largesse? They allowed me to be raised as an orphaned servant boy in my own ancestral home. I supposed I should be grateful they had not had me killed at birth. I was not.

As I lay there dazed in the Forsaken jail cell, I recalled the collision of emotions I'd experienced all at once, outside that door so many years before. I was not wanted by the people who bore me, and I was secretly mocked among the servants I'd always considered my friends. I recall feeling disbelief, outrage, and shame, all at once.

As the servant boy, I was called simply Boy, though I was named Scorfano. As I mentioned, I was not pretty and I never will be. The difference between then and now is that I am secure in the knowledge that the blunt name given me is enough. On that night fifteen years ago, the eve of my thirteenth birthday, when I discovered the truth about my lineage, I holed up, an unwanted animal, in my own head. And it was in that cold, rock-walled cave of anger that I dwelt for years afterward.

I made up my mind that night that I could not spend another night of my life under that roof. Since they who were my family did not want me, I did not want them. Except for a few souls about that Virginia estate who had always shown me kindness, Witter the stableman among them, I was not of that place and owed no one there a thing. Indeed, I justified my next moves based on the notion that it was they who owed me.

I took payment for my shame and humiliation in the form of items that might prove useful to me. From the kitchens, I made off with food, and from the stables, a sheath knife, a broad-brim hat, a coat, and a horse to carry it all, plus me, as far and as fast away from there as I could make it run.

I put that hunter through its paces for weeks following my departure. I suspected they would not follow me because they would be glad to be shut of me. One less horse in return for such a bargain would be tolerated. I hoped.

Because I was large for my age—nearly a grown man's height, though it would not be for another four years before I reached my full height of six foot four and full size—I was able to pass for a young man years beyond my true age, if I kept to myself and kept quiet, averting my eyes from others.

This was easy to do because I had no intention of getting to know anyone personally ever again. I had been treated ill and the singular embarrassment that comes with discovering such duplicity stung like nothing else. Intellectually I fancied, not wholly wrong as it turns out, that I was the match of many men I might encounter. I had been taught to read at a young age by

24

Mimsy, for despite her "cursed desire for the drink," as she called it, she was as much a mother to me as anyone had ever been.

She was Irish born and bred and had a deep and abiding love of books, and she passed that to me. I read and reread everything in her own meager collection, and because she was a well-liked family retainer she was allowed to borrow books from the family's vast library, books that she passed to me to read.

By the time of my departure I had read most of the works in that special room, a feat I'll wager those who dwelt in the upper halls to this day have not equaled. All that reading put me in good stead for a great many situations I was to face in the following years.

It was in this manner that I was able to survive so handily on my own with little molestation. It was also this behavior that kept me from forming any lasting friendships with anyone. A monkish mode of living served me well and appealed to me. I took to the singular life of a lone traveler on the open road as a colt takes to running. I scissored my wandering legs wide and covered a great deal of earth, fascinated and afraid all at once.

This was before the long and hellish war that gutted the nation, and the West was a place of grandeur and awe well beyond the Mighty Mississipp, as I'd heard so many people refer to that flowage. Early days into my journeying, a talkative fellow with whom I reluctantly shared a campfire one evening outside of Saint Louis, said, "The great open West is a place where a man might lose himself forever." I slipped into sleep that night with a smile on my face for the first time in many years. I knew where I was going and I knew what I wanted. I was heading West and I would lose myself there. Forever.

I am still trying to do that. The war did more than delay my excursions, it nearly put an end to them. I did my best to remain impartial, but I could not. It was a complex war fought for valid reasons on both sides, but oppression of one man for another man's gain was and is a repugnant notion to me. So I found myself wearing blue in the conflict, though even there I was a man apart from the rest. The intervening years have only served to accentuate the differences between me and my fellows. And I wouldn't have it any other way.

I lay like that, bouncing from thought to thought, in and out of sleep, for an eternity. The wet, slapping cough of another cell's occupant pulled me finally to a state of wakefulness. I saw, fingertips pressed to my temples, arrow-straight shafts of early sunlight wheedling their way into a barred window set in the wall at head height. I closed my eyes and waited for the inevitable rattle and clang of cups on steel. I didn't have long to wait.

I cursed myself for dwelling too long on unimportant matters and pushed slowly on weak arms to a sitting position. Despite my precautions, my dim but visible surroundings lurched and shifted as if I were viewing them from atop a green mustang. The spot above my right ear was fire to the touch, swollen and jellylike. It would take time healing.

The image of the brown-coated man danced in my brain and helped me regain perspective. The others, the dandified man and his equally tarted-up, fat female companion, were obviously either mistaken about me or hucksters of the lowest order. Was it merely that I am a stranger to Forsaken and that I look the part of a lout? Or was there more to it?

What had been different about my day? Certainly the only answer there was Thomas's recognition of me for whom I used to be. Those people did not seem familiar in the least, and so I must assume that they want something more, something to do with Thomas himself, perhaps? Then why would the brown-coated man warn them I was on my way outside? That had little or nothing to do with Thomas, surely. And why go to great pains to accuse me of a crime, unless it is an elaborate trick to get me out of the way?

All of this pointed back to Thomas. He had said something in the street, something about needing help. Was he truly in danger? Why hadn't he told me?

I cursed myself again. You idiot, Roamer. Of course he'd been trying to tell you, but you rebuffed him at every turn, refused to listen, refused to let him speak. It could well be those people were the danger, and did not want competition for his attentions.

I needed another conversation with Thomas. I had more questions than answers and I felt confident he could fill in some of the blank spaces in my thoughts. Before that could happen I had to deal with the pesky problem of being jailed.

Again, I didn't have long to wait. Keys rang together like it was raining coins outside, and into the cell block hallway stepped Thomas, my little brother.

"Scorfano!"

He stood next to a thin old man with a tarnished star weighing down the breast pocket of a rough-cloth shirt. Next to him Thomas looked like a visiting dignitary, out of place in his starched white shirt and black-and-gold-trimmed brocade vest. Amazing. At that distance, and coupled with one whopper of an aching head, his garb was annoying.

The thought occurred to me then that I may have ultimately gotten the better end of the stick in this deal—I could have been raised to wear such foppery instead of the more comfortable, practical raiments of a woodsman.

They advanced on my cell, and the old man said, "Back off'n the door a bit, fella." He worked the keys in the metal lock, clanging and jangling, and swung the door wide. He held an ancient cap-and-ball pistol trained on me, so I stood in the middle of the cell, my hands to my head, and waited for someone to tell me what was going to happen next. I sure as hell didn't have the strength to make anything happen.

"Surely you don't need that," said Thomas, nodding at the outdated cannon in the man's gnarled old hand.

"Can't hurt."

"But he's free to go. I've paid the fine, and the lady withdrew her accusations."

"Man in a jail cell is a prisoner till he ain't."

"He's right, Thomas," I said, the sound of my own voice cracking and ringing in my head like an echo in a box canyon. "Will someone tell me," I continued, in a near whisper, "what I was accused of having done?" I touched my rubbery head with tender pats.

No one spoke. Not that I cared. Even the silence was painful. I wasn't particularly pleased to hear the woman had withdrawn her accusations, whatever they might have been. After all, there had to be a reason, but I wasn't about to make an issue of it . . . yet.

One step at a time. I needed to get out on the street, head for the livery, then to freedom. The sooner I hit the trail heading northwest, the sooner I could forget about Forsaken and the young dandy facing me. I kept my mouth shut and toddled down the dim hallway.

I was buckling on my gun belt in the outer office before I gave in to my curiosity again. I am nothing if not persistent. "Why?"

"Pardon me?" said Thomas.

I knew he was busting to tell me something, anything, about his rescue of me, but didn't know where to begin.

"Why did she decide I didn't attack her?"

"We came to an . . . agreement."

"What sort of agreement, Thomas?"

He didn't answer me right away.

"What was the agreement, Thomas?"

He looked at me and there was that little-boy shine, as if someone set a diamond glinting in his eyes.

"It was all quite odd, really. It seems they didn't realize you and I are old friends. Apparently the fact that I am, as the kind lady put it, a gentleman, well she naturally assumed that my vouchsafing for your presence with me was sufficient to convince her she was mistaken. The unfortunate aspect of all this is that I still don't have a way through the wilderness myself." He dropped to silence and admired his reflection in a half-shaded window. Subtle, he is not.

I knew what was coming even before I had the opportunity to talk myself out of it. "No. No, you don't." I set my battered hat gently on my head. "How much did you pay for my freedom?"

"Pardon?" He ignored the question and turned this and that way, straightening his cuffs and smoothing his black sleeves.

"I said, how much?" and pulled my coin pouch from around my neck where it hung, tucked under my layers of shirts and buckskin. It was limp, much like my spirit. So, I'd been robbed, to boot. I gritted my teeth and vowed, after I dealt with Thomas, to brace the marshal. Fat lot of good it would do me, I knew, but a man is nothing if he doesn't try in life.

"Scorfano. I don't want your money," said Thomas, showing me his pink palms.

"That's good, because it appears I am now penniless." I glanced at the bemused lawman. "Now, how much do I owe you? I'll raise it soon enough."

He sighed. "I'd rather have your ear for a few minutes. I have a proposition for you."

Now it was my turn to sigh. I figured I had more reason to do so than he, considering my head felt like the inside of an exploding cannon barrel. "Thomas. It's been nice to see you,

29

but I have to leave. In case you hadn't noticed, I'm not wanted in this town and the feeling's mutual."

Before Thomas could reply, I turned my attention to what passed for the law in Forsaken. "Where's my money, Marshal?" I jiggled the limp coin purse. As I suspected, that rat-faced lawdog was as useful as tits on a bull.

"I got no idea what you're on about, mister. But I'm tired of listenin'. If you keep it up, you'll be wasting a length of new rope before nightfall." He jacked a shell into a carbine and bounced a stream of soppy brown spit off the side of a filthy brass spittoon on the floor. I bet his aim with the gun was better. At least at this range.

"I won't forget this, Marshal," I said, staring him down. I've often found that small men are big on attitude, and he was no exception. As he withered into his chair I told him I'm long on memory, if not on funds.

The loss of the coin purse's contents didn't alarm me much. I have a few gold pieces secreted here and there about my gear, for times such as these. It would more than cover my livery bill. But I don't like to be robbed any more than the next man. And especially after an unjustified clubbing, itself the result of some shady deal I hoped to get to the bottom of. And, like it or not, it was becoming obvious that Thomas played some part, unwittingly or no—I'd yet to determine that—in this odd game in the midst of which I found myself.

Of course I still wanted Thomas to go away and leave me alone, but as someone with a knack for pointing out the obvious once stated, "Beggars can't afford to be choosy." I sighed and followed the little whelp out the door, each step rattling my aching head like cannonfire.

On the boardwalk out front, Thomas folded his arms and for a moment, with him standing there in a pouting pose, I was back in childhood and he was trying to coerce me into filching a pie from Mimsy's sideboard.

"All right, Scorfano. I understand. I am only too glad to know I was able to help my friend when he needed help most. It was my pleasure. Perhaps we'll meet again someday."

I made it as far as the livery office, intending to retrieve my horse and gear. I could tell by his shadow in the street that Thomas had followed. I stopped, my hand on the door latch. "What is it you need from me, Thomas?"

Not for the last time did I think I should have kept walking.

CHAPTER FOUR

Some time later, I had finished my meager shopping and was busy squirreling away my purchases in the oversize saddlebags I'd made myself some months before. They are commodious affairs, smooth on the inside and hair-on hides on the outside, made from the skins of longhorns I'd helped wrangle. When all my gear's loaded, there is still room for more, the way I want it. It's also the way I try to end a meal, be it around a campfire or a table in a roadhouse.

It's a habit I adopted years back, when a wise man once told me, "Always leave the table thinking you could eat more." He was a tidy old gent who, though he had little in the way of possessions and even less food, nonetheless shared a fine meal with me when I was a stripling on my way West. His thinking, I believe, was that a man would do well to always leave room in life for the unexpected. I also think his slice of folksy wisdom had as much to do with humility as it did with a decided lack of fare. All I recall of him was his name, Walter. He seemed ancient to me then, and that was a good many years ago. I expect he's dead now.

With that dour thought, I tied off the last of the bags' rawhide thongs and ran a hand along Tiny Boy's massive muscled neck. He gave me a slight nod and one casual glance from his near eye. The big Percheron had been with me a long while and I hoped that would not change for some time to come. A man such as myself has to work hard in this life to turn up as good a companion as a smart horse.

I seldom spoke to him, but we communicated plenty. Nods, glances, the vague but comfortable habits of camp. The quiet reassurance of the familiar is enough. At least it is for me. Tiny Boy has yet to complain. I've told him he's free to leave but he goes where I go, and vice versa.

My old chum, Maple Jack, is forever haranguing me about taking on a pack animal. I tried it once and found I accumulated possessions just because I had the space in the panniers to fit them. But it never felt right and flew in the face of the simple, straightforward manner I endeavor to live my days. The less I have the more I am.

I say such things in Jack's presence in part to rile the old goat. It works, every time.

"You mean to tell me you wouldn't like more room for books and such?" He's dumb like a fox, is Jack.

The man knows my armor chinks. But he'll have to work harder to convince me I need another mule or a horse to lug my gear. Tiny Boy is anything but what his name implies. He's built for steady, determined effort, and his broad, muscled back can hold a sight more than I load him with. Even when it's me he's toting.

But in the spirit of fairness and equality among trail chums, I keep my gear to a minimum and walk whenever it's possible for me to do so. It's good for me and good for the horse. A shared smiling temperament makes life on the trail a more pleasant undertaking.

I glanced up the steps toward the mercantile. Thomas had been in there since we parted on the street before the livery. He was set on "outfitting" himself, as he kept referring to it. You'd think he was planning a trek to the deepest reaches of the Dark Continent instead of a week's ride northward to visit what he had told me was a "prime ranchland property" purchased by his father. That his father was also mine—something of which he was unaware—and that Thomas believed himself the sole heir to any and all fortunes the pater had left in his scurvy wake was not lost on me. Nor did it impress me.

As I have said, I care little for owning property, and even less for the leavings of a man of our father's distinct lack of worth. Harsh words? Yes. Earned by him? I choose to think so. I would never utter them to Thomas, though. To him the man was, however flawed, his father, his own papa. It is not my place, nor will it ever be, to dissuade him from those beliefs.

Since he never received anything resembling a guiding presence in his life from his father, and since he considers me to be like an older brother (the boy has never been more correct in his life), I feel beholden to him in this respect. Enough so that I begrudgingly agreed to help him find this mysterious ranch.

I asked him for details but he pulled that annoying smirky smile, the one he straps on once he has received what he wants, and told me all would be revealed in good time. Each of his numerous anger-inducing traits as a child flitted back to me like early-season biting midges in the high, wet country of the northwestern coast.

He has no idea how close I came to reneging on my offer. But I am a man of my word, so I suppressed a growl and told him I would meet him in front of the mercantile in thirty minutes. That was—I looked to the sky fruitlessly, but clouds obscured the sun, appropriate for such a foul burg—coming on toward an hour and a half ago. I wanted to get out of town, knowing the marshal wasn't keen on me, a mutual feeling. I wasn't certain I could trust myself if I saw him. He had, after all, filched my cash while I was out cold.

Mostly, though, I wanted to get shed of Forsaken because it was like every other town I've ever been in—filled with people who look at me as if I had gutted their favorite dog with a wooden spoon. I sighed once more and clomped on up the steps to the mercantile. I gave one last look up and down the street for sign of the woman and two men from the day before, but saw nothing of them. I had not expected to, but that didn't mean they were gone from my mind.

The springing brass bell tinkled above my head as I opened the door. The weather was well into autumn, it being September 20, and no one was particularly happy to heat the outdoors, as Jack says when you open his cabin door for any reason at all between September and May (no matter if he does spend most of his time crouched around his outdoor fire pit, cooking, brewing coffee, and holding forth on every subject and then some).

And there was Thomas, decked out in crisp new duds more appropriate to the local farmer's sensibilities and wages than what I imagine he hoped he looked like—a trail-hardened drifter. At least he'd gotten rid of those dandy togs he'd been wearing. Though they weren't far—a hint of blue and black caught my eye and I saw his fancy clothes folded in a stack, that god-awful hat atop, down the counter past stacks of goods.

He turned to me, a wide smile on his face. "Look," he said, gesturing with a pink, soft hand at the new goods as if he'd carved each and every box, tin, and sack out of raw rock.

I nodded. The shopkeep eyed me over half-moon spectacles jammed tight on the long fleshy bridge of a nose that ended in a knob of warts. At least I wasn't alone where hard looks were concerned. He went back to licking his pencil nub and tallying the motherlode of a purchase. Crimson spots on his veined cheeks told me he was determined to squeeze every last drop out of Thomas's wallet.

I walked to the counter, looked over the goods. "Thomas, some of this"—I nodded toward the laden counter—"won't be useful to you, especially on the trail."

"Nonsense," he said, dismissing me as if I were an annoying

fly. Why even ask me for help if he knew what to bring? I held my tongue, not wanting to endure another of his pouts.

"Have you procured suitable mounts for us?"

"Not sure about us," I said, "since I have my own horse. But yes, I did as you requested and bought a decent horse for you, a fine buckskin—"

"Yes, yes, but a second beast as well?"

"I was getting to that, Thomas." The tightness in my voice made them both, Thomas and the shopkeep, look at me. My voice can be as big as I am, though I try to keep it reined.

"It's a solid pack animal, a Morgan cross, I'd guess. Sure-footed."

"Two saddles?"

Now I was plain confused. "No, well a riding saddle for you, yes, and a pack rig for the little horse."

Thomas sighed, looked at the shopkeep as if to say, "Look what I must endure." Both men shook their heads and surveyed me, the apparent simp.

Thomas went back to primping his collar, then plopping one hat after another on his head as he looked in a small clouded mirror. "Didn't I mention? There will be three of us all told. You, me and . . ." He did not meet my eyes in the mirror and certainly did not turn when he said, "The girl."

"What girl?" My witty response for the day.

"Why . . . Scorfano, didn't I mention it? Ah." He smiled and turned back to the mirror. "Must have slipped from my mind. But yes, her name is Carla, ah, something or other. We met on the stagecoach to here from Green River, I believe. Seems she is traveling alone, poor little sparrow, to her father's ranch. Her escort went and got himself arrested in some unpleasant place, and she had no choice but to trend forth into this brutal wilderness all on her own."

"What's her father's name?" I asked, knowing the answer

before he shrugged. "Did she tell you the name of the ranch?"

Another shrug.

"Okay then, where is this little lady now?"

"She's at the hotel, of course. Her escort, the cad, the scoundrel, stole all the traveling money her father had wired her to make the journey."

I nodded, suppressing yet another sigh. I had a feeling I would be doing so a whole lot in the coming days. "I take it you are her new escort."

CHAPTER FIVE

Something about this Carla girl seemed familiar. But it wasn't the girl herself I recalled, rather the type of person she was—a grubber. I knew as soon as I saw her eyes, pretty green eyes, to be sure, but no smile in them. There was at once so much more and so much less to her than Thomas supposed.

The boy's obvious wealth, which he took no pains to disguise, made him an instant target for scoundrels. And I've learned over the years that those in society who ply the swindling trade come in all varieties and can be men, women, young, old, it doesn't matter.

As for the rest of her, she was the sort of woman who rarely has to rely on her wits, as her pretty face, atop a body to match, would make that pursuit unnecessary. She wore a smile that was as false as the hard edge in her eyes was true. Her gold hair, streaked throughout with chestnut as if painted in, sat coiled atop her head and pinned neatly beneath a tidy feathered red appurtenance doing little to earn its worth as a hat.

She wore a dapper red wool riding outfit, pleated skirt and jacket, beneath which poked ruffled lace cuffs and collar. Her boots were not meant for riding, but square-toe button-ups, black, with squat heels of little use in a raw mountain landscape.

Pointing out to Thomas that she was a digger of gold, namely his, would be impossible. I took small comfort in the fact that at least I would be along to keep an eye on the smitten fool and the pretty woman who, I bet myself a penny, was out for his dollars and little else.

"Carla, Thomas tells me you are the daughter of a rancher from north of here." I patted Tiny Boy's neck. He flicked an ear, moved little otherwise. "Good lad," I said, then looked again to the girl. "Whereabouts is the ranch? I've spent quite a lot of time roaming this range and never tire of finding new folks."

She didn't respond right away. I waited, and, forgive me for saying so, but a smidgen of myself enjoyed watching the war between truth and lie in her veiled eyes, enjoyed watching the slight twitches on her cheeks. She knew then that I was on to her fraudulence, but as soon as Thomas piped up, a catlike smile emerged on her pretty pink lips.

"See here, Scorfano, there's no need to pester poor Carla. Can't you see you're making her uncomfortable? How would you like it if—"

But I had already walked away, headed for the livery. "Come if you're coming," I said, leading Tiny Boy. "Your horses are waiting."

"But my purchases!" shouted Thomas, his yelping stopping a few folks on the wooden boardwalk fronting the scattering of buildings that made up the downtown of Forsaken.

"Bring them along," I shouted back, smiling to myself. I really can be an ass sometimes. But only when I've been hoodwinked and lied to.

It took another half an hour to wrangle with the livery owner to take his old packsaddle back in trade for a riding saddle suitable for the girl.

"No sidesaddle business here," he said, before splattering his own boot toes with a sloppy stream of chaw spittle.

"No matter," said the girl, showing off a split skirt for riding. Her method of doing so was bold enough to widen the old man's rheumy eyes.

"Yes'm," was all he said as he bent to the task of rerigging the little horse.

It took far too long to load the foolish amount of near-useless gear Thomas had purchased, which included duplicates of the few vital cooking accoutrements I already told him I had—a fry pan, a coffeepot, two tin cups—his set of four would at least be useful for the girl, and on and on.

Well past the noon mark, our sorry little pack train, of which I was reluctant leader, trudged out of town. I think Tiny Boy was embarrassed. "You and me both, boy," I said, patting his girthy neck.

"What's that you say, Scorfano?"

"Nothing, nothing at all, Thomas. Let's make time while the horses are fat and happy, eh?" I tried a smile as I looked over my shoulder at them, but the girl's eyes may as well have been daggers. And from the way Thomas bounced and jounced in the saddle, it had been some time since he had ridden a steed under the watchful eye of someone who knew of such matters.

I was about to offer him words of advice regarding sitting a saddle when it occurred to me he would likely end his day in bowlegged pain, his privileged backside aching something fierce. As I said, I can be a stinker when I've been crossed.

We rode for many hours. The waxing moon, pinned high and bright, cast light enough for us to follow the established wagon trail well into that curious time between day and night. A half hour after we cut to our right, headed northward off the trail, I halted Tiny Boy in a pleasant glade of rattle-leaved aspens not far from a rushing brook.

I turned once more to check on the progress of my companions and was surprised to see Carla not ten yards behind, and though I could not make out the look on her face, I bet it was a smirk of satisfaction. Of Thomas, there was no visible sign, though I was not alarmed as he made noise aplenty. His moans, which hours before he had abandoned any hope of disguising, were piteous and shameful.

I faced forward once more, indulged in a full-on smile, and toyed with telling them that we were but two hours from our intended camp site. I did not scratch that itch. Best to parcel out one's pleasures as one may in life, no matter how petty or paltry.

"We'll make camp here. Give the horses a good rubdown, feed, and watering, then tend to our own needs." That was greeted with a mixture of relief and moan from Thomas, who slid from his horse and stood sagged against it, spraddle-legged and whimpering.

"Ah," I said, stretching my shoulders. "But there is nothing like a leisurely horse ride through mountain passes in autumn. Gets your blood up, it does." I was laying it on thick, trying to sound like Maple Jack. But that is a fool's errand, as no one can do that save for Jack himself.

"Where are we headed?" said the girl.

"Why, that's what I was fixing to ask you, ma'am. You see, I can't get you to your father's ranch if I don't know where it's located, now can I?"

But she didn't rise to the bait I cast out there. Instead she turned to soothe the blithering of Thomas. I may or may not have whistled a little tune while I tended to Tiny Boy. "If you think you're up to it, Thomas, you might want to gather firewood. We'll all appreciate your efforts once the cool of the forest settles on us."

To my surprise, he nodded. "Yes, you're right, Scorfano. I'll see to it."

"And me?" said the girl.

"Well, let's see," I said. "If it's not too much trouble, you could tend to your horse, then Thomas's. You'll find nose bags in that canvas pannier, along with oats. We'll hobble them yonder." I nodded toward a grassed patch to our right, silver in the moonlight. I was not sure if she saw where I'd indicated, or even if she cared.

Later, as we enjoyed coffee, eggs, and salty ham steaks around the fire, I almost allowed myself to feel, if not happy about the situation, at least more comfortable with it. Almost.

I sipped my cup of coffee, suppressed a belch, and said, "It is time, Thomas, for you to share details of this journey with me."

You would have thought I had asked him for all his money, and his hair, too. But something happened that I should have predicted, but hadn't. The girl spoke up.

"Do let's hear the particulars, Tommy." Carla blinked big doe eyes at him, a smile raising high the corners of her pretty mouth.

To my knowledge, she was the only soul who had ever called him Tommy. Smitten as he was by her it didn't bother him.

"Oh." His own smile appeared and as if he were offering some great indulgence to poor folk everywhere. Thomas sat straighter and cleared his throat with great ceremony.

I almost rolled my eyes.

"My father"—he turned to the girl—"was a well-known raconteur and master of high finance." He winked at the girl. I wondered what the significance of that wink was. Could it be that Thomas knew what a seedy rogue the old man was? That he had squandered not one but two family fortunes in whoring and gambling and in making anything but clever decisions where finance was concerned? That he had convinced his equally shifty wife to shun his oldest child?

I concede on one point: He had enough of the milk of human kindness in his black heart to allow me to be raised as a stable boy by the old family retainer, Miss Mimsy. How thoughtful of him, this paragon of virtue Thomas was so busily genuflecting before in conversation.

Bah, but I am allowing bitterness I had thought well tamped

and all but dried up to bubble once more to the surface. It appears the sores of my youth are nothing more than old wounds that scab over but remain in a state of fester beneath. Will this be a lifelong affliction? I hope not, but time is a slow and confounding healer.

"I have on my person the deed to a sizable property, a ranch, or so I have been told, purchased with the last of my family's fortune. It was my father's dying wish that I assume the mantle of patriarch of my family, only fitting as I am the oldest male and sole heir. He wished me to make something of myself in the wilds of this vast Western place."

Thomas paused to sip his coffee, allowing this scant information to settle on us like a scrim of gauzy fog. As for myself, the news of my father's death announced once more bothered me little. The man meant nothing to me, even if his mistreatments carry long weight.

"What of your mother?" said Carla.

"Ah, yes, she is gone as well, and I am an orphan in this world."

The girl uttered a forced sob and clutched at his arm. He patted her hand, nodding his head in sorrow.

"I am . . . sorry for you," I said.

Thomas eyed me with curiosity. He suspected I was torn up somehow by the news, that I was hiding it. In truth, I felt as little at the news then as I had when he'd told me the day before in the bar.

"This ranch property," I said, clearing my throat. "Do you know any more about it than the vague details you've shared with us?"

"Oh, please, sir," said the girl, stiffening as if I had slapped her. "Can't you see Tommy is distraught?"

"It's all right, Carla. Scorfano is correct to assume I should be more forthcoming with details of this venture. Suffice to say all will be revealed as time rolls on. For now, Scorfano, I wish to remind you that you are in my employ and will guide me north-westward. Soon I shall share more of the details with you. For now, please be patient."

"Employ?" I wanted to drive a fist into the middle of his smug face. "I don't recall any talk about pay for my services."

His eyebrows rose and the girl smiled. She was enjoying herself.

Before he could stammer another annoying word, I satisfied myself with a grunt and left the fire to tend to the horses. I suspected they had botched the hobbling and feeding. Why did I have the feeling, with each word he uttered, that I ought to leave him now while he could still find his way back to Forsaken?

CHAPTER SIX

We closed in on Maple Jack's wilderness kingdom late the next afternoon as the day's light once again commenced its vanishing act. We all three were tired and I know at least two of us were sore from the saddle, and I wasn't one of them. That at least provided small comfort.

It pained me to bring them there, to share anything of my life with Thomas, let alone the conniving girl. But I had a few items Jack was looking forward to, not the least of which were cornmeal and whiskey, two items the codger did not like to survive without. He was quite capable of doing so, but he was not a pleasant fellow to be around at such times when one of his fritters hadn't clogged his gullet or the fiery liquid he so enjoys hadn't passed his whiskered lips.

I also wanted his read on the peculiar situation. I pride myself on being an insular sort, living for months at a time alone, away from the hubbub and clamor and annoyance of other humans. I have much to learn and only someone as grizzled and traveled as Maple Jack can teach me, as coarse and cobby as he appears to most folks.

We rode single file winding upward, picking out the trail that is no trail, as Jack prefers it, between boulders and thick Ponderosa pines. We topped out along a ridge in a glade overlooking a broad natural meadow that rippled gold in the autumn afternoon's light.

I was about to say, "Well, we're here," when a voice boomed

at us from a half dozen yards to my right.

"Where'd you conjure this motley assemblage from?" The voice was soon matched with a face.

"Forsaken," I said, offering a smile. "Howdy, Jack. Good to see you."

"And you, Roamer. And you."

His squinty stare eyeballed the two stunned whelps in my wake. He would know, of course, that I would not have violated his privacy by bringing strangers here had I a reasonable alternative.

"Forsaken?" he said, snapping the silence like brittle kindling. "What a rat hole of a town. Only worthwhile beast ever crawled out of there was a cur with hydrophoby. And that had the good sense to die when it got itself shot—though it took two bullets. Critter was deranged beyond compare!"

He let his proclamation of the fetid town, an estimation I could not argue with, settle on us like cold drizzle. Then he smiled. "Present company excluded, of course." He strode down the slope, colored beads and metal trinkets dangling from his buckskin garment's fringes, clinking and tinkling as he walked. "Do let me help you down, ma'am." He held up a calloused hand more accustomed to brain-tanning hides than assisting damsels.

Carla, who despite her hard edge had moments before been poised on the verge of tears, now blushed and placed a tentative kid-gloved hand in his paw.

That was Maple Jack, all over. Speechifying, as he calls it, one moment, and the next doling out big helpings of his sunbeam smile. I've rarely seen anyone who can stay angry with or confused by the man for long.

He made us welcome, bustling about the place, cooking and muttering and smiling and whistling and sampling the jug throughout it all. I helped work up an impressive feed, contributing as much of Thomas's purchased victuals as Jack would allow—never an easy feat when he played host.

As for Jack himself, he ate nothing, drank coffee laced with jug juice, and said he'd fire up his skillet later. "Still full-up from a sizable midday feed. If I'd known to expect visitors I would have held off." He cut me a quick look and guilt winced my face.

In such a manner the evening aged, and full dark found us all relaxed around the fire and dozy. Jack insisted "the lady," as he referred to Carla, spend the evening in his cabin. He and I would sleep by the campfire out front, the spot he spent much of his time in all seasons but high winter storms. As for Thomas, he trailed into the cabin after Carla, red in the face and muttering something about making sure she would be comfortable and had everything she needed.

From my spot at the fire, I made out Jack's back as he exited the cabin. He leaned back in. "And no hijinks nor patty fingers! You keep to your sides of the cabin or you'll feel the almighty wrath of me. You ask Roamer, I ain't one to be trifled with." He clunked the door shut and made barely a sound in his moccasins as he padded his way down the worn path to the fire ring.

He winked as he sat down with a sigh. "I think they're too tuckered out for horseplay. That boy ain't like me, I'll tell you. Was a time I would sidle on up to a pretty little girl like that, grouchy old man nearby or no!" A low rumble of a laugh boiled out of him and he nodded toward the skillet. "How's my pan heating up?"

"Just fine—nearly there."

"Good, got to be hot for beaver and onion."

I stretched my legs out toward the fire and ran a hand gingerly along the side of my face. Earlier, while fetching water from the creek, I had seen in my reflection swelling and purpling along my cheek and on up the side of my head. Whoever clouted me, likely that nasty little marshal, hadn't taken any chances. Can't say as I blame them. There isn't a person I've come upon who isn't convinced my homely visage rides ramrod on every Wanted dodger from the mighty Mississippi to the Cali coast.

Okay, maybe I'm feeling a little simpery, as Jack would say, but a man gets weary of false accusations. And the bruises to my bean don't tend to help the matter any.

"Roamer."

Jack always does that, says my name, then waits, eyeballing me, whenever he wants my attention. I left off rubbing my tender head and looked at him.

"I am too polite a man to have asked you when you wandered on in here earlier, but . . . how in blue blazes did you get conked on that big shaggy bean of yours again?"

"Two guesses, first doesn't count," I said. I sounded surly. Didn't mean to with him, the man to whom I owe so much, beginning with my life.

Maple Jack sighed. "You got a right to be in a grouch, I reckon, what with being mistaken for a outlaw at every turn in the road. But confound it, boy." Jack swigged from his jug, dragged a grimy cuff across what I assume was his mouth, buried as it was somewhere in that bushy tangle of beard. "Why don't you up and let them have it for once?"

It was my turn to fix him with a steely stare. "And how do you expect me to do that when I'm unconscious in a jail cell?"

He grunted, swigged again, which was his way of saying that he didn't have a ready answer, but would soon enough. I didn't have long to wait. "Oh, sweet sufferin' hogwallows!" He chucked more onion slices into his fry pan. The man likes his onions. He waited until they were skittering and popping in the bubbling ooze of bear fat lining the bottom of the cast-iron pan before he spoke again. "I expect asking you to give up on your wandering ways is like . . ."

"Like me asking you to set fire to this place and take to the trail."

He grinned, squinting through the smoking mess that was his onion-and-beaver fry-up. Beaver, in case you were wondering, is pound for pound the most healthful of all meats you are likely to come across. Has a whole lot more to offer than a cut of thick elk flank. Or so Maple Jack says.

Me, I'd rather have the elk steak. I've tried beaver on several occasions, each time to humor Jack, and each time I come away feeling as though I've tangled with a snake-oil cure-all for everything that has ever or will ever ail me. Except the rampant galloping gut-runs that fried beaver seems to bring with it.

I'm not convinced Jack comes away any less afflicted, though he would never admit it. He'll take his firm beliefs to the grave. Dedication to conviction, in my estimation, is an admirable trait in a man. Doesn't mean I have to agree with him, though.

Jack all but licked his plate—not that he would do so. The man is coarse but couth, if that makes any sense—belched, and patted his puffed-up belly. "I'd say the kiddies are retired for the night." He nodded toward his cabin, from which we'd heard neither peep nor shriek. I believe I rode them too hard, and being green as a pair of summer apples, it wore them out, or at least their backsides.

"What say we get down to it."

I set aside my plate. It seems I had managed to work on a slice of beaver after all. "You mean about Thomas?"

"And that young lady, Carla. Though that's the kindest remark I can think of to say about her. I'll warrant she has rascality on her mind." He set fire to a wad of tobacco in his apple-bowl pipe.

"She claims to have a ranching father somewhere north of Forsaken."

"Bah, she's out for the boy's money."

After a few quiet moments, I said, "That young man"—I watched the orange-black pulse of the coals—"is my . . ."

I let the word hang, could not seem to drag the rest of the sentence up out of my tight throat. Up until that moment I believed my thoughts on the matter were little more than a scarred-over nub of hard flesh without feeling. But I could not say "brother."

Once more Jack rescued me. Big old me.

"You've shared your past with me," he said quietly. "I can guess who the lad is." He worked the stem of his pipe in a circle about his face. "More of a resemblance than you might think. It's in the eyes." He winked.

Neither of us spoke for a few moments. A dry branch cracked in the fire, surrendered to flame, sending bright sparks pluming.

"He know?"

I shook my head. "Still treats me as an old acquaintance, a hired hand, nothing more."

"That set with you?"

I nodded.

"What's he looking for out here then, if not for you?"

I sipped my coffee, steaming from its spot on the rock at the fire's edge. "He claims to hold the deed to ranch land, also north of Forsaken."

"Convenient."

"Mmm," I said. "Needs someone to guide him to it."

"Well now that could be over Pascal Valley way. Nice open country with a fair number of ranches."

I nodded. "That's what I was thinking."

"Ranch land that way could be worth a heap." Jack wasn't looking at me, but I knew what he was thinking.

"I'm not interested," I said.

He leaned forward. "But you're the rightful heir, not that pup."

"Keep your voice down, will you?"

He let it drop. For a few seconds. "You want a hand wrangling them two youngsters?"

"It's not just them." I sighed and told him about the three strangers in town, the woman and two men who had caused me grief. That perked his ears.

"So that's why you agreed to escort them on this jaunt to the great unknown."

I nodded. "As near as I can figure those people got wind of the property and would like to own it themselves. Of course, I'm guessing. I'll squeeze Thomas when the time is right. The whole notion felt hinky enough that I wanted to get him out of town as soon as possible. Then the girl stepped in and complicated the proceedings."

"Womenfolk will do that. So you think that girly in there is in cahoots with them?"

Again I nodded. I'm nothing if not consistent. "I'm not sure how yet, but it's a safe bet."

"You'd best let me come along. You'll need the help."

I said nothing, knowing Jack had plans to travel eastward over the Bitterroots to visit friends north along Salish Lake. He'd visited that country more than a few times in recent years and I had a feeling it was something other than the fertile shores of the lake that led him there. He'd told me a few months before when I'd passed through this way that he'd be venturing there this autumn. I hadn't wanted to bring Thomas or the girl here, but if I had passed by I would not have seen Jack before he left.

"No, I'll be fine. They're harmless, the others, too. Likely little more than coyotes sniffing at something they thought would be easy pickings."

Jack and I both knew I was full of hot air and little else.

51

Thomas was a gullible fool, and the girl a bugbear at best. If she was more than that, it would be revealed sooner rather than later on the trail. I hoped it didn't involve those others from town. But I'd be damned if I was going to let this silly little escapade interfere with Maple Jack's life.

"Tell you what," said Jack, smacking his hands on his knees. "We'll sleep on it, have another quick palaver in the morning, once we get ourselves on the safe side of a stack of flapjacks."

Just like Jack to put off until tomorrow what could be decided right then and there. He sat down with a grunt and groan on his blankets and laid back. "And don't burn 'em," he said.

I smiled, laid down on my side of the fire and wedged an arm under my neck. "Night, Jack."

"Yep."

I saw stars through the tall pines, winking as the branches swayed in a high-up breeze. Other than the two headache-makers in the cabin, the evening was as I always enjoyed with Maple Jack—quiet conversation around the campfire, rounded off with a hot meal, bubbling coffee, and a few pages in a book I'd not yet read.

I peeked over at my saddlebags, within reach, but somehow didn't feel like cracking open my latest indulgence, a fine used copy of the book *The Pathfinder*, a sequel to James Fenimore Cooper's excellent *The Last of the Mohicans*, a book I have enjoyed several times over the years. It would wait. I wanted to savor the words, not read them with half my attention.

Jack's steady crosscut-saw snores threatened my eyelids with a weight I did not yet want. I had thinking to do. But I was quickly losing the fight. The last I thought I heard as I slipped into sleep—excepting Jack's grizzly-rattle snores—was a sound from the cabin.

My eyes snapped open, and sudden clarity bloomed in my mind. I'd been a fool, lulled into believing the girl was more innocent than she really was. I'd left her shut in with Thomas, the whelp I'd vowed to protect. I stood and made my way up the path toward the cabin. It was slow going as I did not relish barking my knees on a stump or a rock. Some distance from the cabin I heard a muffled squeak as the door opened.

"Thomas?" I whispered, hoping it was him and not the girl. I repeated his name.

"Yes?" He walked a few steps down the path toward me. "Is that you, Scorfano?"

"Yes." I saw him clearer, the moon lighting the cabin grounds well enough to get around without a lamp.

"I woke because I have . . . well, I have to relieve myself. Does your friend have an outhouse?"

"Not as such. Choose a tree."

He didn't move.

"It's okay, Thomas. There's no critter mean enough to trespass on Jack's place. You'll be safe." I tried to keep the grin out of my voice.

He nodded, offered a weak smile, then ambled off in the dark, still obviously in pain from the long day in the saddle. He chose a Ponderosa not too far from the cabin. In daylight that would have been an awkward spot, but I didn't bother him about it.

Greenhorns, I thought. Then a cascade of embarrassing memories washed through my mind and I realized I was being unfair. I had, after all, been greener than a spring sprig when I'd come out here. I reckoned I was still feeling surly.

He came back. "Well, good night again, Scorfano," he said.

"Just a second," I whispered, then beckoned him to follow me further away from the cabin.

We were halfway down the trail to the fire when I stopped. "I'm thinking, Thomas, that it might be best for all concerned if you bunk down by the fire with me and Jack, give the girl her privacy."

He drew his head back as if I'd smacked him across the face. "Scorfano, I'm not sure what you think has been going on in there—"

"Keep your voice down, and your righteous rage tamped down, too. I only meant that it would be the gentlemanly way to behave, after all. And you are nothing if not a gentleman." I figured stroking his silly strutting ego could round the edges off my suggestion.

"I know your intentions are nothing short of fully honorable, and I'm certain she feels the same." I had no confidence in that little lie, but I plowed on ahead with my wobbly logic. "I'm thinking not only of her reputation, but yours as well. Imagine if it somehow got known that you had spent the evening with the girl in a dark cabin. All alone, the two of you. Hmm." That set him pondering, alarm raising his eyebrows.

"Quite right, Scorfano," he said, nodding with vigor as if it had been his idea.

I ushered him down to the fire, where Jack was still sawing big logs into small logs like the old pro he is. I handed Thomas my top blanket and he wrapped himself in it, unaware it had been mine. In his eyes it was nothing less than something he deserved.

"Look, call me Roamer, eh? I've gotten used to that. The Scorfano name is . . . that kid is no longer. I'm not that person, haven't been for a long time. Okay?"

"But you'll always be Scorfano to me."

"Well, that's fine, but call me something else, anything. Even 'Hey, you' would be better." I tried to make my request sound casual, but the damn name annoyed me, still does. I wanted it good and dead.

"Okay, Scor—, I mean Roamer. Okay. Good night, then."

"Good night, Thomas."

"Oh, for the love of petunia! You two shut your maws," Jack piped in, his eyes still closed. "Or I'll stopper 'em tight with hot cinders."

In the dying firelight I saw Thomas's eyes widen as big as hen's eggs. I stifled a smile and rolled over.

CHAPTER SEVEN

The next morning found me up before Jack and Thomas, and from the sound—or lack of it—before the girl, too. I stalked into the woods toward the stream down below Jack's place to relieve myself and freshen up for the day's ride. There was a chill tang on the air, different than most autumn mornings, something to think about. Snow? Perhaps. We were in high country, after all. Snow certainly was due any time from then to late May, in my experience.

As promised I made flapjacks, using Maple Jack's time-trusted recipe, something he held in high esteem, as it had been his mother's. Jack cooked out of doors much of the time, all of it, I believe, save for deep winter storms when venturing out is an impractical matter. I followed suit and in no time had tin plates piled high with tasty sourdough flapjacks.

True to his word, Jack also had a supply of syrup on hand, though from what trees he procured the sap I know not. The man's ways remain mysterious.

The meal and our cleanup was a quiet affair with little comment from anyone, least of all Jack. I had regretted bringing them there even before we had arrived the day before, and that hadn't changed.

In an effort (paltry, I know, but I had to do something) to lessen my guilt over the entire odd brief visit, I spent the better part of an hour splitting wood for his fire. I tried to teach Thomas how to use the two-man bucksaw, but his own prejudices against sweat-raising effort in life prevented him from settling into the pleasing rhythm of the clean push-and-drag of sawing. It was painful watching him.

He stood and massaged his hands after a good five minutes of effort.

"Perhaps you could look to the horses, tie on loads," I said, offering him an excuse to leave off the task.

"Yes, excellent. I see you have this well in hand."

I nodded, rolled my eyes when he turned away, and set to the wood with renewed vigor. I took the opportunity to make the saw sing. I am as I am, a large man with a homely countenance. I had little to nothing to do with saddling myself with either of these. But that does not mean I don't put this big body through its paces. I can muckle onto a two-man crosscut saw and use it alone. Such work feels good.

And though I am largely a traveler, and by dint of preference a solo adventurer, I put effort each day into keeping myself fit. On long stretches where gazing at the wonder and majesty of a hidden valley or the far-off peaks of a range of mountains may be fulfilling to the mind and soul, it does little to maintain one's precious machine, the body.

So I do what I must, lugging rocks from one place to another, arranging fallen timber such that I have a cozy campsite for however long I choose. I spend much effort cutting and splitting wood. At such times on the trail, I do not have a saw but an ax, a fine single-bit head with a beefy hickory handle reinforced at the base with a collar of steel.

It is something of my own devising, and I was fortunate enough to have a blacksmith friend of mine down New Mexico way fashion it for me. As to another blade, I have a tomahawk for splitting kindling and for defense. It rides on my waist at all times, as does my Green River knife.

This little recollection has strayed me from my path, another trait I admit is a product of keeping to myself for much of the time. When given the chance I am a windy fellow. Or perhaps, on reflection, it is from spending so much time with Maple Jack in my formative years. If he is any indication, there are worse ways to be.

Jack had never protested when I set to a pile of wood. In fact, if he wasn't right there with me, grunting and swinging an ax—his is a menacing double-headed tool more suitable for wielding by some unspeakable creature in an old Norse tale—he will sit down on a stump and criticize my sawing or splitting techniques. The man is not afraid to vocalize his thoughts.

On this morning, he kept to himself, tidied up the campsite, and acted odd somehow. It was noticeable only to me, as Thomas and Carla did not know him. Finally, there was little else to do but load up and head toward the vague destination Thomas had in mind. That was about to change.

"Before we continue this little game, Thomas, I need to know particulars of the journey. I'll need to see your deed, something with a reference to a location. Otherwise we are wasting our time."

Along about that time, Jack piped up. "That's right," he said, a horned old hand roughly patting the neck of Thomas's horse. "How do you know where you're going if you don't know how to get there?"

That said it about as good as I could. Unlike Thomas and the girl, I hadn't yet mounted up. I stood beside Thomas's horse and held out a hand. All was still for a few moments, then Carla said, "It seems a reasonable request, Tommy."

He sighed, slumped in his saddle, and reached into an inner coat pocket. It was buttoned and took him a few moments to undo. At long last he retrieved a thick sheaf of papers, the color of fresh cream. The outermost sheet bore elaborate scrolled writing of a fine hand, and a narrow wine-colored ribbon encircled the lot. A blue wax seal, stamped with a signet, had been lifted off instead of broken. I saw it had taken a bit of the paper with it.

The documents were of the legal sort, and certainly looked as if they could be the deed he had mentioned. Until that moment, I had doubted the kid was playing straight with me.

Before he laid the papers in my hand, he hesitated, looked into my eyes as if he wasn't sure he could trust me. What was the root of this suspicion, this fear? As obvious and juvenile and confounding as he could be, Thomas could also be inscrutable. Dumb like a fox, Jack had said about him the night before.

I doubted Thomas heard Jack and I talking, but did the young man have his own suspicions of our relationship? None of it mattered much to me then. I only wanted to get down to the business at hand, that of determining our direction and destination.

As soon as he laid the papers in my hand I folded a thumb over them and slid them free of his grasp. "Thank you, Thomas."

He made to speak, and I cut him off. "I need this only to determine our direction."

"I was merely going to tell you," he said, adopting his nasal tone of superiority, "that the map, such as it is, is the third or fourth sheet in the stack."

"Okay, thank you."

And he was right—there was a map, such as it was, boldly drawn with remarkably little detail. But it did offer a series of north-south jags in black ink, labeled in red ink as "bitter roots"—a mangled spelling of the range along which we were traveling. Good. To the west spidered blue scattered threads I took to be rivers.

Jack crowded close and I lowered the map so we both might inspect it. In silence I dared Thomas to protest. The only sound I heard was the girl fidget, offer a slight sigh as if the entire affair was boring her to no end. Two peas in a pod, I thought. Perhaps they were destined for each other.

"There," said Jack, tapping a grimy finger on the map. "That there's the Salmon River. Recognize that pointy bit anywheres. I was nearly killed by a mama grizz and her three cubs one fall, oh, about this time, must have been a dozen years back."

The girl gasped, put a hand to her chest. It seemed a genuine reaction. I'd heard the story, though when he told it to me the first time, the mama grizzly had been a black bear with two cubs. Richer with age is how Jack liked to describe most anything in life. Said everything worth knowing or doing or hearing should get richer with age. I can't argue that point.

Thomas and the girl both stared wide-eyed at Jack. Perfect for him. I resumed studying the map while Jack spun a windy. Soon enough he got his arms into it, proceeded to dance around in a circle, mimicking the attack, the growls, the screams of agony, and generally described the tussle with as much color as he is able—which is saying something. The man can tell a story.

"Grabbed me right here, by the back of my neck, hadn't been wearing buckskins I might have lost my head right then and there."

I suppressed a snort.

"Something you need to add, Roamer? I don't recall seeing you in that river valley, do I?"

"No, sir. I was nowhere to be found."

"That's right, you were a squallerin' bairn, I reckon."

Thomas spoke up. "But Mister Jack, I thought you said this took place a dozen years ago, surely Scorf—, ah, Roamer, was around these parts then?"

"A dozen, two dozen, I don't rightly recall, young man. You see, when you're being dragged in your buckskins by a brute of a silvertip sow, and her half-growed cubs are gnawing your toes and fingers off, you don't think to consult a calendar! Now, where was I?"

It was Carla's chance to pipe in. "You were being dragged."

"Yes, that's right. Thither and yon, as the fancy men say, thither and yon."

Again I chuckled, to myself. I'd not heard Jack use those particular words. Could be he'd been saving them for a special occasion.

"Why, whatever did you do, Mister Jack?" It was the girl again, following Thomas's lead and calling Maple Jack *mister*. I knew I would have fun with that at a later date.

"Do? Do? Why, I didn't do a damn thing, you'll pardon my vocabulary, dearie. Ain't much a man can do when he's being dragged by a brute of a bear—one of the biggest in the northern range."

"But how did you escape?" said Thomas.

"Didn't," said Jack, looking back to the map. After a few beats, he said, "Died right there." He tapped the map, didn't crack a smile, didn't look up, but ran his finger along the blue line.

I certainly didn't smile—Jack can deliver a quick shot to the shoulder that would fell a strong man. Experience is a harsh teacher.

Well north of the blue line that held his interest, though south of Coeur d'Alene, sat a star with the words *Rawlins Hall* beneath, in neat black hand, scripted small. I flipped over the stack, looked at the outer, thicker sheet of paper that acted as a cover for the rest. There were the same two words, though in that elaborate scroll, and followed with the word "Holdings."

Neither Thomas nor the girl spoke. They sat stunned, eyes wide, unsure what to think of the story or the man who told it.

"About like we thought last night. If that star is your ranch, laddie?" Jack looked up at Thomas.

"Yes, the other papers indicate that Rawlins Hall is the name of the estate."

"Estate?" Jack and I said the word at the same time.

Estate is a word rarely heard in the west. Usually it's ranch or tract or some such. "Exactly how big is this 'ranch' you've inherited, Thomas?" I said.

He glanced at the girl, then down at us, and he blushed. I didn't think it was a possibility, but the kid blushed. "I . . . I was only trying to use the parlance of the West, Scorfano."

"How big?"

"If the deed is correct, and I have little reason to doubt it, then it is substantial. But as to how many hectares or how much acreage is involved, I do not know specifically. It's only given in measurements that are tricky to decipher. They are in miles and sometimes in feet, sometimes in rods, sometimes measured in days' rides. It is all rather confusing. But it seems large."

"Sounds like you got yourself quite a mystery to solve, boy!" This Jack said to me, then slapped me on the shoulder and walked over to the campfire to refill his cup. "You best get to it—I'll be thinking of you when I'm snug and warm in my winter wickiup alongside Salish Lake. Heh heh heh."

I scowled, and didn't try to suppress it. I tucked the sheets back in on themselves into their accustomed folds. As I tied the ribbon, I said, "Do the papers offer more clues as to the location of this . . . estate?"

"Yes," said Thomas, looking slightly less red about the face.

I handed them back to him. "Good. We'll consult more later, once we've gotten some miles underfoot." I mounted up and looked at the girl. "With any luck we'll make it to your father's ranch today. Be sure to let me know when we get close, eh?" I winked at her and nudged Tiny Boy into a walk.

"Jack." I nodded toward my old mentor.

He did the same, said, "Roamer." That was about all we ever did by way of farewell or greeting.

Little did I know all our lives were, in short order, about to become a ball of woolly yarn all but impossible to untangle.

CHAPTER EIGHT

The morning's promise evaporated as the sun rose and the trail took its toll on Thomas's constitution, notably his sore backside. There was little I could do for him save call an end to the cause of his misery, but I was not about to slow our progress, let alone stop, not before dark neared. Autumn has an annoying habit of filching hours of daylight from us and I wasn't ready to surrender them without a fight.

And that made hearing the youngster's occasional mumbles, which increased to a near-steady burble of whimpers, all the more annoying. I could take no more. I halted the paltry little train of trail travelers and turned Tiny Boy to the side. He tossed his massive head and I did the same, a masculine nod of sympathetic agreement.

"Thomas, if you are in that much pain riding, perhaps you should hop down and walk a spell. I am afraid I cannot slow our pace. Weather in autumn in the high country is fickle, and we don't want to tempt fate by dragging our toes."

His look of annoyance and pain struggled on the edge of anger as he gazed at me. That was not his usual state, I knew. If anything, Thomas was perpetually gleeful to a fault. And too willing to trust, no different than a puppy in that respect. But that point is neither here nor there.

His unexpected rage triggered something in me, something unkind I am ashamed to say, and I shifted my gaze to the girl. "Carla, you have not made half the fuss poor Thomas has, despite the fact you don't appear to be all that familiar with a saddle yourself. Is there some secret you could share with him? Let him in on how you are able to ride without giving in to the agony of the undertaking."

I hadn't spoken so much all at once in a long time. It was cruel of me, I knew, but I wanted to shut him up somehow and shaming him seemed the only way to do it. And it worked—at least for a time. Excepting occasional gasps and grunts, Thomas quieted down. We resumed our walk, with the girl, to her credit, not playing into my pettiness.

Annoyed with myself as well as with Thomas, and with the situation in general, I thought instead of the route we were on. Now that I had at least a general direction, I felt slightly less confused by the entire pursuit.

Throughout the day, the trail wound along the base of the range of foothills that led to the bold, raw peaks to our right, the east. I had occasion to check without seeming to do so on my two charges. And I noticed the girl would, more often than not, be looking behind, at our back trail.

The countryside thereabouts is varied, at once stark, rubbled, and open, then flowing golden with winking tips of grasses coating a rolling landscape that resembles a rumpled blanket. Soon, stalky pines trailed down the flanks of the hills, forcing us onto a jagged route. Glancing behind I caught the girl doing the same, and for long moments, as if hoping to catch sight of someone. Or perhaps she'd already done so and had grown fearful.

Long hours of slow travel, of baking sun, and little conversation could easily have turned her skittish. As likely she was as I had initially suspected, not alone. I had let my curiosity linger too long in gazing and she turned before I could shift my sight. She caught my eye and I nodded, forced a sheepish grin, and looked forward. I hoped she was sold enough on her pretty looks to think I was a buffoon smitten with her.

For his part, Thomas appeared dulled and near lifeless in the saddle. He had even abandoned his whimpers and moans and was now silent. Life on the trail did not appear to thrill him. Yet another trait we as brothers did not share.

I knew I would not sleep that night. If my suspicions about the girl were correct, she had accomplices. For what end? Obvious reason told me Thomas's story still had chapters yet to be revealed—at least to me. But the entire affair had grown wearying. Perhaps it would come to a head soon. If not of its own volition, I would force it so.

New wrinkles or no, I have had enough experience with vicious bastards who will ambush a man for a hot biscuit and a cup of coffee. What did my little party have to offer? And should I brace the girl and force her knowledge from her before an unwanted surprise reared its foul head in the night?

"I see a promising valley ahead," I said. "Should be decent grass for the horses and firewood aplenty. We'll scout it, camp in the trees."

The girl responded with a nod, Thomas with a grateful smile and relaxed eyes. We rode on and in ten minutes reached the spot I'd chosen. It was largely as I suspected, and for that I was grateful, notably for the steepness of the terrain backing it up. If anyone were to launch an invasion from that direction, they would have to be a mountain goat or a winged wraith.

I had already set myself up as a loner—no struggle there—so excusing myself from the campfire with a cup of coffee to sit by myself above the scene would not be awkward. But it would be expected. Then a better thought came to me. I would feign exhaustion and see what came of it, all the while napping like a sneaky mountain cat.

As I picketed Tiny Boy in a sizable grassed meadow well within reach of the stream and ample roughage, I heard the girl whimper. She struggled with her saddle, which I had seen her lug and hoist and slide from the back of her horse with ease several times. "Tommy, oh, I need help. I . . . I guess it's true what they say about women being the weaker of the sexes."

For a man who had been crabwalking about the campsite, doing his best to avoid being useful, moaning and groaning, Thomas all but hopped to her side, laying a hand atop hers on the saddle horn. "Oh, don't say that, Carla. Here, let me help." It was almost embarrassing the way he fawned over her. And all without managing to exert himself much at all. Truly impressive.

Yep, Tommy was good and smitten. Basing it on looks alone, I'd say she was worth being smitten over. But he was blind to what I and Jack saw. It didn't matter to Thomas that she was playing him like a tight-strung fiddle.

"I'm going to fetch more firewood." I slid my ax from its sheath on my gear. "Thomas, why don't you and Carla use that branch there to get a fire going. I could use hot coffee, and I bet you both can, too, eh? Then we'll see about cooking something."

He barely heard me.

"Thomas?"

That time he heard me, and sighed to let me know it. "Yes, yes . . . Roamer." He turned away from me.

He said my name as if it were a foul taste on his tongue. If he was trying to annoy me further, his efforts were paying off.

"Oh, Tommy," said the girl, holding his face between her hands. "Silly boy, he's only trying to help." She winked at me over Thomas's shoulder.

I headed off in the direction we'd come from. I wanted to scout our back trail, and I'd spotted a blowdown on our way in. Mostly, I wanted to be shed of those two, at least for a spell.

I spent the next ten minutes limbing the tree—the dead aspen was dry and gratifying to break up. In no time I had a decent pile of sizable wood I left long for lugging. I'd break it down into manageable lengths once I carried it back to the fire.

I was intent on gathering the firewood and didn't hear the girl approach until she stepped on a twig. I spun, ax gripped tight. She was still a dozen yards from me. Her eyes widened and she held up her hands at chest height, palms outward.

"Carla," I said, looking beyond her. "Did you get the fire going? Camp all set up?"

She kept walking toward me, a wide smile on her face, eyes narrowed as if she were a cat about to pounce. "I left Thomas to deal with the camp. I thought I'd lend a hand with the firewood."

I gathered a pile of it in one arm, sunk the ax head into the butt end of a bigger length, and readjusted my grip on the smooth wood handle. "Kind of you," I said, "but not necessary. I'm set."

She raised her skirts and planted a boot on the log. "Nonsense," she said, still smiling. She slid the skirt higher, up over her bent knee. "At least let me help hack up the smaller branches. Here," she said, revealing a sizable Bowie knife riding in a sheath on her thigh. "I have the tool for the job. Oh, it appears to be stuck in the sheath. Could you . . . would you mind helping me?"

As shapely as the leg was, I am not a fool, at least not at that moment.

"No," I said, taking no pains to hide my disgust with her. I turned and tugged hard on the ax, which was lodged deep in the end of the log. It upset her pose and I heard her stumble. But she was persistent and jogged to catch up to me. No mean task, as I have long legs and can cover ground—even laden with firewood—when I've a mind to.

"I only wanted to help," she said, smirking.

"Uh-huh," I said, ever the master of conversation.

"I bet you're wondering why I have such a big knife, hmm?" She reached out and wrapped long fingers around my straining arm. I jerked it hard and she took the hint. She kept on talking as if nothing had happened. "A girl has to have protection out here in the West, right? After all, I don't seem to be able to count on the men I meet."

I glanced at her, shaking my head but saying nothing. She pulled a pout on her mouth, but her eyes danced as mischievous as ever.

"Your chatter is wasted on me, girl." I stopped, shifted my grip on the ax and wrapped my other arm tighter around the bundle of branches. "I don't know what ploy you are playing with Thomas, but I see you for what you are, don't think I do not. He may be a rube in this country"—I jerked my chin toward the camp—"but that doesn't mean I am. Watch your step with him, you hear?"

I started off again, the quick glance I'd seen on her face gratified me. It was the first time I'd seen her look agitated, worried even. Now I had to figure out what was behind the look.

We made it back to camp without managing to speak. Thomas had also had a victory of sorts—he'd managed to conjure smoke, if not visible flame, in the midst of a poorly assembled fire ring. I almost congratulated him as I dropped my cumbersome load beside the fire, until I noticed the dozen or so snapped and spent wooden sulfur-head matches littering the ground beside where he squatted. He looked like a trained monkey I'd seen once at a drover's camp along a trade route to Kansas City.

My mood matched his. "You went in my bags, I see, and found my packet of emergency matches."

He barely glanced at me. "Yes," he said, wagging his hands feebly at the sputtering smoke he was trying to bring to life.

"You could have made them easier to find. You are the guide, after all."

"Why didn't you use the matches you bought?"

"Oh, did I buy matches? I had forgotten."

Like hell, I thought. Why was he rummaging in my gear? I gritted my teeth and knelt before the dying fire. "Stay out of my traps," I said in a low, menacing growl. "And blow on the damn fire, Thomas. Use all the wind you are full of for something other than idle chatter."

In minutes I had a decent flame licking into the snapped ends of fresh, dry wood. Just as well, as the temperature in the mountains drops quickly once sunlight performs its daily vanishing act.

"What say after we eat we take a look at that document of yours, eh, Thomas?"

To my surprise, he said no. "It will be far too dark by then. I think we should wait until morning."

My attempt at civility stomped on. "Fine with me," I said. "You're the boss, after all." I'd meant it to be sarcastic, but he took it the only way he knew how—literally.

"You can be certain I am in charge of this excursion, and don't you forget it . . . Scorfano." His brief glare at me was hard, barely suppressing further anger. He looked like a small dog, cornered and eager to snap off a poking finger.

That's when it occurred to me that he hadn't liked Carla trailing after me. I don't think he'd seen her rummaging up her skirts for her knife, but I bet myself a whole shiny dollar he was wallowing in the pangs of jealousy. I felt more than ever like a schoolmarm. Right then all I wanted to do was travel to Salish country with Maple Jack. It was the closest I'd ever come to feeling homesick.

We ate in silence, and cleaned up the same, despite the girl's attempts at chatter.

"I'll take first watch," she said.

"Oh no, I'm fine," I said, standing.

"No, no. I insist. It's the easiest watch, after all. I hate waking in the middle of the night." She made a quick mistake then, involuntarily, considering how she usually conducted herself. She glanced over her shoulder, again toward our back trail.

"Well, if you insist. Never let it be said I fought with a lady." I stretched and feigned an exaggerated yawn, but inside I was smiling.

I looked at Thomas, but he was pouting, and hadn't a clue about chivalry. Just as well. I wanted to keep an eye on them both. His little snit would all but ensure he wouldn't try to sidle up to her out of my sight range. Even as I thought this he laid back on his blanket, pulled another over himself, and closed his eyes. I know he was tired, because I was, and I was more suited to life on the trail.

The girl was too eager, too willing to take on the watch.

I followed suit, stretching out on my own blankets further from the fire. "Now Carla, you'll promise to wake me at the first sign of trouble." I'd already spent our first night on the trail explaining the importance of spelling one another in shifts to keep an eye on our animals and gear.

"Why?" Thomas had asked. "I can't imagine there are all that many travelers out here."

"No," I had said. "You're right. Though the ones who might come along could as easily be angry Blackfeet or Sioux as itinerant gamblers down on their luck and eager to fill their pokes with easy pickings."

He'd shuddered, the effect I hoped my words would have on him. "But the real culprits will likely be of the four-legged variety."

They'd both turned confused glances at me.

"Wolves, mountain lions, bears."

"Snakes?" she'd asked.

I nodded. "Yep, they're around, too."

Thomas had blanched at the thought. "How do we . . . keep them away?"

"You don't," I'd said, spreading thick the dollop of fear and enjoying it perhaps a bit too much.

And so now, a handful of nights into our journey, we were divvied up as we had been, though I usually took a couple of watches and nudged Thomas into action. This was only the second watch the girl had taken, and the first she'd volunteered for. I offered up one last grizzly yawn, rolled onto my right side with my back to the fire, and pretended to collapse into a deep slumber.

It took longer than I expected before I heard the sounds I expected, if that makes sense. I remained on my side for a couple of reasons—I could keep my eyes half open without danger of being caught at it, and I kept my ear cupped toward where the girl had positioned herself, dimly visible ten yards away at the periphery of the firelight's glow.

Laying on my side was also mighty uncomfortable for that long, and so would keep me from truly falling asleep. It was akin to a trick I'd been told by Maple Jack that Indian warriors used the night before a big hunt or battle. To prevent oversleeping they would drink a fair bit of water before they retired. Their discomfited bladders kept them from lazing in bed.

As I said, I ended up waiting longer than I expected. But it had been worth the wait. As near as I could figure, I lay that way longer than an hour, taking care to breathe deeply, and even offer up the occasional rattling snore. I am no stage actor, but I fancy my efforts were believable.

Eventually the girl stood from the boulder on which she'd perched, and wandered further into the night. Our fire had all but died out, only glowing coals remained. The night was a cool one, though not nearly as nippy as I had expected.

At least I wouldn't be easily seen as I rolled further from the fire. I kept low until I could be certain I was in total darkness. Each move I made had to be thought out—one snapped twig or scraped bit of gravel and I'd be sunk before I floated.

I paused, heard nothing but genuine deep breaths from Thomas as he dozed in complete peace in the land of dreams. The little greenhorn lived a magical existence—never seeming to want for much, always getting others to do for him what he could and should have done for himself. I was as guilty as anyone else for falling into his smiling trap. Still he snored on.

I didn't have far to go to hear whispers. Was the girl talking to herself? No, even though I had expected to hear voices, the stranger's voice still came as a shock. I had hoped my guesses were incorrect. But the girl was in league with scoundrels.

I edged closer, closer, and the whispered murmurings became clearer, words, hushed but hurried, became distinct words: ". . . papers . . . no chance . . . big oaf." That was the girl, then a second voice, a man's, said, ". . . no time . . . but we'll wait . . . morning soon enough . . . no later."

I leaned closer, planted my fists before me on the ground— and quickly snapped a stick in two. Big oaf, indeed. The voices stoppered as if corked in a bottle. I held my breath, and after what felt to be an hour, the voices resumed, though lower. I could make out no more words.

Presently I heard a lessening of words, and suspected they were finished with their nefarious plotting. I retraced my knee-walking route back to my blanket, some yards behind me.

Thomas still slumbered, oblivious to everything. I was never further from sleep. I barely made it back under my blanket when the girl walked close. My hand rested atop my Schofield, ready to draw. Though if she had a weapon drawn on me, I doubted I could clear the holster in time.

I couldn't chance that she'd not seen me as I rolled into my blanket, so I said, "Hey Carla. That you?"

There was a pause, then she said, "Yes, I . . . sorry to wake you. Just coming back from a . . . a call of nature." Her voice sounded timid, even in a whisper. She suspected I'd overheard.

I'd keep an eye on her—and one on the entire camp, to boot, for the rest of the evening. Daylight couldn't come fast enough for me. I needed to get Thomas away from her, alone, to figure out the rest of his fuzzy story. There had to be more to this deed than he was letting on. It would not surprise me to learn there was more to it than he himself knew.

I sat up, made a show of rubbing my face with my hand. "You get some sleep. I'll take my watch now." I stood and heard no protest from the girl. That's because, as her companion had whispered, the morning would be soon enough.

For what, I would soon find out.

Something tickled in my mind—that extra sense Jack says develops when you have been a long time alone, traversing the wild places, with little more for company than your thoughts. I suspect he's talking about instinct. And my instinct was telling me to beware—murder was in the offing.

Of course, nothing else of note happened that night. Not that I wished it to. Still, I kept my eyes and ears alert to every rustle in the fallen leaves—I was grateful it was autumn. I heard each snort from the horses, each light snore from Thomas, and each slight breath from the girl, who settled down closer to Thomas than I would have liked.

It took another hour—which put us but an hour or so from dawn—before I was convinced she had truly dropped off to sleep. I let the fire die out completely, preferring not to be sky-lined against any light a barely tended fire might have offered.

I rose to my feet, my right knee popped and strained, and nearly gave me away. I'd wrenched it not but six months before in a rock slide while being chased by a handful of testy Blackfeet. But that's another story for another time, as Jack says. The knee hadn't yet healed, at least not well, and likely would not ever return to its youthful spry condition. It was loud enough that the girl rolled over in her sleep. I paused and waited for her breathing to even out.

All I wanted to do was find a tree to lean against and let my body do the rest. A man's latrine duties aren't something to trumpet about, but I wanted to get that morning ritual over early so I could keep an eye on Thomas. I figured since they were both asleep I could safely risk a predawn visit to the bushes. I was wrong.

I made it to the privacy of our downwind-from-camp latrine, little more than a cat hole. By then gray morning shadows were emerging from the blackness of full night. I gambled I would be out of sight of the camp for a couple of minutes at most. I should have held it.

CHAPTER NINE

It was the girl's voice, oddly enough, weepy and desperate, that woke me. Rather it roused me from my dazed state. I don't think I'd been asleep so much as unconscious. My first clear thought was that I'd taken another nasty knock to the bean. I could only imagine what a laugh Jack would have once he found out.

My vision was a blurred mess, and didn't get better as I squeezed my eyes and tried to focus them. Something was in them, or on them. I shook my head—a mistake, as a sickening dizziness further confounded my addled melon.

I was aware of a noise, a voice, other than the girl's, bubbling through pond muck. It was my own, trying to speak, trying to make any familiar sound. Breathing was forced and shallow, I wasn't getting enough air. Felt as if I had a mouth full of wool. Then something ripped and popped, and sweet, cold air rushed into my mouth, filled my windpipe, my lungs. I gulped like a beached fish.

Another something rapped me hard on the side of my head. I fell over onto my shoulder. Whatever was on my face shifted. Now I saw better than I had. I blinked again, several times, looked up and saw full daylight. I squinted—a man stared down at me, he looked familiar somehow, tall, leering with a full set of teeth too big, too bright for a mouth. And all set in a long, pulled horse face. Lank hair, brown, I think, wagged to either side of his face like wet yarn. The mouth said something. My ears weren't working well, once again. The words came to me as if through mud.

Then he bent out of sight, reappeared, and I saw the canvas water bucket hove into sight, a wash of water followed it and whatever fuzziness plagued me snapped straight up and out of me.

"Gaaah!" The only sound I made for a minute or so. I looked around as noises came to me, more distinct now that the clanging bells in my head receded as if heard from across a plaza instead of nested in the belfry.

Thomas sat a couple of yards from me, his arms awkwardly held behind his back. Ropes lashed around his middle, looped around his legs bent before him, and ended wrapped a number of times around his ankles.

He stared at me, eyes wide, a grimy red bandanna holding a wad of grimier cloth stuffed in his mouth and tied tight around his face. The veins on his neck stuck out like fingers and his face was a red, puffy mess. Tears washed down his cheeks and snot strung from his nose. He'd never looked so bad, but it was his eyes that plagued me.

They stared right at me, the eyes of a five-year-old-boy tagging along behind me all those years ago, begging me to play with him. And if I didn't indulge him he would lapse into heartfelt tears, and I would catch hell for not tending to my chores. He didn't ever know, would not have cared, but I could not let him down. And I never had.

Until now. Damn kid and his pleading eyes. What had I done? More to the point, what had I not done?

Guilt and anger washed over me as I turned to face the toothy, stringy-haired stranger. He was laughing at me, braying like a donkey. I blinked hard, rubbed my face against my shoulder and found I could not move my own arms. I was as trussed up as was Thomas. My ankles, too.

"What have you done? What do you want, damn you? Tell me now!" I had intended my words to sound menacing, but they were rubber, toothless.

Through it all the girl sobbed and simpered, standing beside the donkey-sounding man.

"You told me no one would get hurt! Don't hurt them, stop it!" Her words had no effect on him.

That's when I saw the other two, a slender man, on the short side, sporting fancy whiskers, and a fat-faced woman. I recognized them straightaway—the devils from the street in Forsaken. The damn bloated cur who'd accused me of accosting her, the one who'd got me tossed in jail overnight on no evidence, the one who'd gotten me robbed by the lawman. So they were without doubt the ones following us.

What I recognized next changed everything. The fat woman wore a distinctive fur hat, a tawny affair with black speckling, proud-crowned and blocked oblong. It bore a triangular snout flattened across the front, widening with the face fur of the handsome lynx it had once been. Two pointed ears, tipped with fine black hairs, jutted from atop.

The back sported the nub of black-tipped tail of the same beast. To my knowledge there was only one such hat in all the world, and it belonged to Maple Jack. He'd made the hat himself, of an animal he'd not wanted to kill, but had been forced to. Another story for another time. But the hat was not something he wore every day. It was something he saved for "steppin' lively," as he put it.

It was also a garment he would never, ever give up while breath still filled his old lungs.

"What have you done to Jack?" Even as I bellowed it, my words becoming less muddy with each breath pushing them out, I saw other of his possessions. The skinny, bewhiskered man wore Jack's beaded knife sheath and his homemade Bowie skinner. He'd looped the belt knife on a thong about his skinny neck. The elaborate beadwork on the buckskin sheath, a gift to Jack from the Flathead battle-widow he had kept winter company with for some seasons now, was as distinctive as was the lynx headpiece. And another item he'd not part with by choice.

"What have you done to Jack!" I barked it again, this time not as a question but as a rage-filled demand. I blinked away blood and somehow struggled to my knees, despite the tight hemp ropes lashed about me like a snake bent on strangling me. They cinched my waist, my arms behind my back, then down to the wrappings around my ankles.

The horse-faced man drew a massive revolver—it, too, looked familiar. And I knew it for what it was—Jack's old war Dragoon, practically a blunderbuss.

The girl screeched, lashed out at the man. He took a slap to the face and kept on smiling. The woman pulled the girl off roughly, flung her sprawling backward, but I didn't care what happened to her. My concern was for Thomas, for me, for Jack. What a mess.

I tallied my situation, the odds of accomplishing anything other than getting myself shot, and figured I had the worst odds in the history of games of chance. But what was the alternative, Roamer? I asked myself. Lay low and do nothing? This horse-faced fool had murder on his mind, and I was not about to let him scratch that itch without trying something, anything.

I funneled that pure, eye-shaking rage into forward action, rocking and balancing on my knees. I hoped there was enough play in the rope for me to stand, at least tall enough to launch myself at the homely lout, to use my head as might a mountain ram in battle.

I calculated I had one, perhaps two seconds before he pulled the trigger. He still had to cock the big gun and that was a chore in itself. But my maneuver up off my knees was not so simple or straightforward as I wanted. I made it up off my knees, but the ropes, bound too well, were more than I could stretch, let alone snap. I shouted at the killing muzzle of my best friend's revolver, and beyond it, the long, grinning, toothy face of my killer.

The gun belched fire and burst with the sound of five train-wrecks. Someone shoved a full-grown tree straight into me. I saw blue sky, the tops of bare trees, smelled the raw stink of a fired gun, heard screams of horses and people as if they were clashing with an orchestra from the netherworld. Then my sight once again blurred, I tasted the bitter tang of metal in my mouth, and I knew no more.

CHAPTER TEN

"This ain't your day, boy."

So, I thought to myself, that's what the voice of God sounds like. Nothing too special about it. If anything, it sounded familiar. Then it fizzled out again.

"You hear me, Roamer? I said you have had one rum run of luck."

Something nudged me in the arm. It took a few moments of effort, but I came around.

The voice spoke again. "Course, so have we all."

I kept working on opening my eyes, they felt crusted shut from something—blood? How was that possible and where in hell was I? I recalled Thomas, the camp, the girl, the whispering, tied up, the two, no, three evil visitors . . . a wild cat? A lynx? Jack's lynx . . . Jack's knife, Jack's gun! I had to be dead, shot at close range with that ancient beast of a revolver.

"What . . . hap—"

God's familiar voice cut me off, stomped right on my words.

"You're a lucky kid, have me stop along like this. Why, for all you know I could be a thief, a professional gambler, out looking for a stake in the wilderness. But—"

It was my turn to cut him off. "Jack? That you?" My words slurred, ran together.

I heard a rustling sound, then the voice drew close, spoke to my ear. "Course it's me, boy, who'd you think be fool enough to trail after you?"

I still wasn't convinced. Couldn't be him. "God?" The word fell out of my mouth before I could stop it.

God laughed right then, and I knew it wasn't really him but Maple Jack. I also knew I wasn't dead. At least not yet. It was a mighty effort to open my eyes. One stuck, but the other popped open. I saw little. "It night?"

"Yes, it's full dark, boy."

No wonder I couldn't see so well.

"How long . . . I been out?"

"Long enough for me to get worried, then give up on worry. You been out a day, near as I can figure." He touched my lips with a tin cup and I sipped. The water tasted so good, felt so good I gulped, lashed at it with my tongue, spilling it on my chest. I didn't care.

"Go easy, boy. You been hurt bad. Ain't out of the worst of it yet."

"What happened?" I said, forming mushy words to match my muddled thoughts.

"You been shot. I scouted the tracks some, but—"

"Thomas?" I said, cutting him off again, twitching, trying to raise myself up on my elbows. It was not one of my better-thought-out plans. Pain lanced me like lightning bolts thrown from the skies thrown hard at me.

"Near as I can tell he's alive. Was when they left here. Why else take the whelp?"

I said nothing, so Jack continued. "Scouted here, saw tracks of two men and two women, one of them that fancy girl your brother dragged along, the other a heavy-set piece of work. She leaves big prints. A third person, had to be Thomas, left nothing more to read than drag marks. That's how I suspected it's him they took along. Cowards, except the boy, of course."

My mind was filled with all manner of foolish thoughts tumbling on each other, one after the other, like puppies in a basket at the market, jostling for attention. "Your hat, gun, knife . . . I saw them."

"Oh, good. I wondered if anything made it out."

"Out?" I said. "What do you mean?"

Not but a couple of feet away, I saw a figure lit by the campfire, a yellow edge outlining him. It was Jack all right, but something was different. Something about him seemed . . . off. I tried to make sense of it, tried to find a way to ask him something, anything, but sleep dragged over me like a thick blanket and once more I was adrift, a strange, inky current tugging me far from what I knew.

When next I came around, it was full light out. I felt horrible. All over. My head thudded as if it was filled with unending cannon fire, and my body felt much the same. Then I tried to move.

I'd made it halfway to raising myself up on one elbow when someone shook the earth, spun it in a joking cosmic fashion. A flood of dizziness welled up, broke through my weak self, and threatened to drown me once more in blackness.

Jack's voice came to me again, clearer with each shout. The man is persistent.

"Roamer! Boy—stay with me, you hear?"

I tried to say yes, tried to say anything, but only mustered a weak forward movement with my head. It was enough to stop Jack from shouting, and to rally the cannons into a fresh volley.

Much as I appreciated that man's doglike persistence, it was fraying my nerves to near snapping. The swirling abated, along with Jack's voice, and I risked opening my eyes again. Slowly at first, then wider as nothing worse happened.

"Jack?" I croaked. "Water . . ."

He looked down at me. Once again I only saw his outline, this time, though, it was the bright sky behind him. He left, then returned a few moments later with the tin cup filled with water. He held it to my mouth and I lapped at it like a dog.

"Easy now, easy, boy."

He was closer to me and I remembered what I'd thought hours before when I'd last been awake. My old friend looked different somehow.

"Jack," I said. "What happened to you?"

"Oh, weren't nothin'. Don't worry about it. Get some sleep."

"No, no . . . tell me."

Jack closed his eyes and sighed, then sat back on a log. That's when I got a good look at him. He looked mighty rough—his beard, normally full and fluffy, that he kept mostly clean, was singed and matted along one side, as was his hair. His face along the other side wore a cluster of welts where the skin had blistered. His prize buckskins bore rents and slashes. Blackened spots showed he'd been through an awful time. He was also wheezing as if from exertion.

"Jack, what happened? You look like you've been dragged through the gates of hell."

He grinned, nodded. "Yeah, just about."

I struggled to sit up, made no progress.

"Okay, okay, don't get your bustle in a crimp. It was three rascals, a woman and two men, who come along a day after you all left. I seen 'em coming, but they looked harmless. I had 'em set themselves down by the campfire and I offered to make them coffee. They said they'd sure appreciate it, as weary as they were. Told me they was from back East. No kiddin', says I." Jack laid a grimy finger alongside his nose, winced as he accidentally poked his blistered cheek.

"I went up to my cabin to fetch my fancy guest cups, you know them new tin ones? Been a year since I had occasion to use them, then all in one week I have two reasons to drag 'em down off'n the shelf. Anyhoo, I turned around to come back out—mumbling as I am prone to do when I have too much on the fire and no way to tend it all."

Jack stretched his legs, took on a thoughtful look, then resumed his story. "I try to be a decent host, but I didn't have time enough to wrangle all manner of visitors. I was set to head out the next morning up to Flathead country, don't you know.

"Rummaging as I was in the cabin, I wasn't paying enough attention to my guests. That's when I heard a scuffing sound from the doorway. I looked up and there stood that homely fat woman. A harder-looking face on a female I've rarely seen. Looks like she's been used as a chopping block, then soaked in brine and gnawed on by porcupines."

That about matched my memory of the woman who'd been wearing Jack's knife—the same beefy cur who railroaded me back in Forsaken.

"She was in the doorway, twitching her eyes left and right, looking about the place. It's a mite dark in there without a light, as you know, but I'd seen that look plenty of times before in my travels. A digger looking for goods for the taking. 'Now see here,' I told her. 'I got my guest cups but there's nothing in here you need concern yourself with, ma'am,' I said to her. I always try to be polite to the ladies, even when they have a face like a mud fence.

"Well, she put her hand to her big ol' bosom, you know the way a woman will do when she feels she's been wronged, though in my experience that means they're playacting, and she says to me, 'Why sir, I have no idea what you mean by that.'

" 'Well, ma'am,' I said. 'Maybe yes and maybe no, but I have the cups and you all were kind enough to offer up your own coffee beans, so let us adjourn to the campfire. Might be I can help you with your directions and your map.' That was something they'd asked about when they first bothered me."

Jack leaned toward me. "But do you know what, boy?"

I shook my head slowly, the cannons still going off in random, thunderous volleys between my ears.

"That hard-looking woman tried to block my path, my own path leading from my own doorway to my own firepit! You might have gathered by now that I had a lot on my mind, for I am usually quicker on the draw than that. I said to her, 'Now, see here, ma'am, I ain't up for games. I am about to depart on a journey and I have chores to tend to.'

"She all but manhandled me! I pushed past her, and I no sooner had set foot out the door when I was attacked by her companions. Them two bounders tucked right into me with fists and foul breath and kicks and punches. As I mentioned, I was busy and not in my right mind, else I would have laid those buffoons out cold, I tell you. But they got the drop on me, and next thing I knew they'd trussed me up tighter than bark on a birch. I didn't go easy, though. I lay there all roped, not unlike how you looked when I come upon you. Only I was squallerin' like a riled grizz cub.

" 'You will regret this, curse your foul hides!' I shouted all manner of oaths, some of them not fit for a woman's ear, I will admit. But then again she was about as far from a woman as you are likely to find and still be one, if that makes sense."

I nodded, hoping he was going to come to the pointed end of the story soon. But you can't rush a raconteur like Maple Jack. It's akin to pulling the Dutch oven off the coals before the biscuits have cooked.

"I heaped all manner of curse upon them, all the while trying to reach my sheath knife to slash those ropes—then I recalled I'd not strapped on my weapons that morning, as I had intended to don my traveling togs before the day was through, that way I'd be ready to hit the trail when I woke, you get me?"

Again, I nodded.

"Good, now here's where it gets interesting." Jack leaned forward, eyes wide.

CHAPTER ELEVEN

The closer he got to me the worse Maple Jack looked. What in the hell had happened to him? He looked like a bear cub I'd found half dead after a forest fire. Its hair had been a blackened, pasty smear. Jack's eyebrows and some of his beard and hair bore the same look. The rest of it was still wild, as usual, sticking up even when a hat was thrust on it.

"You know what those rogues did? They rummaged through all my worldly goods, took what they wanted, unbundled everything I'd packed up to take with me, and tossed the rest thither and yon like there was a cyclone in the cabin. Soon enough they all three came back out, stood looking down at me in the dirt.

" 'What do you want now?' I said, eyeing them. 'Seems like you got my goods, you vile, thieving so and sos!' "

Jack winked at me. "Those weren't my exact words, Roamer, but I am not certain you can take a dose of my full verbalizing, given your weak condition.

" 'Where's your horses at?' said one of the men, a rangy-looking varmint with a big, long face like a swayback old plow horse.

" 'Ain't got no horses!' I shouted, which ain't no lie, as I only have Ol' Mossback, my mule.

" 'You expect me to believe that, you rank old critter?'

"That's what he called me! Me! You believe that, boy? I am one of the most tidy persons you will ever come across in all your life's travels, Roamer. I wash pretty near every week, whether I need it or not." He nodded, not requiring my response, so convinced was he of his cleanliness. Truth is, Maple Jack can at times be hard on the nostrils, especially if you're downwind of him. But I am not about to utter a word to him on that score. I have been on the receiving end when his dander's up, and when he's irritated he's like a crazed bantam rooster flying full in your face.

"The man commenced to kicking me with those stovepipe boots of his, the dog ears flapping in time with his kicks. They didn't hurt none, except where he snapped a few ribs." Jack rubbed his torn, blackened buckskin shirt above the rise where his belly paunched out. Then he groaned for effect.

"What happened next?" I said, wanting to know the story as much as he wanted to tell me. He grinned, his eyes sparking like flint scraping steel.

"They all three muckled onto me then, and you know what they did? They tossed me like a log for the fire right back into my own cabin! 'Well thank you very much!' I shouted, 'For seeing me to my own door and then through it, besides!'

" 'Shut up your yapping!' that horsey, toothy bastard shouted, then they slammed my door and I heard them jam something in front of it. At least I'd be shed of them quick, I thought to myself, laying there in my own cabin, all trussed up, stoved up, and bruised and bleeding, too. But I knew where I had a old hatchet leaned against my wintertime fireplace. For kindling. You know the one, you've used it enough. Never have I seen a man big as yourself, Roamer, need to make more fuss over kindling.

"Where was I? Yes, yes, in the dark in my cabin when I heard their voices outside, first along one wall, then from another, then up on the roof as well. 'Now what do you suppose they are up to, Maple Jack?' I said to myself.

"And I answered myself, though only in my own head, because you get yourself locked up for talking to yourself. At least in a town, that's my experience, anyway. My old, dear, sainted mother back in the hills of Vermont always talked to herself, though, and she ended up all right. Said you meet a better class of people when you natter on with yourself. So I do it, too. Then I tell you what happened next."

Jack leaned forward again, and whispered, "I smelled smoke!"

"They fired your cabin?" Given his singed appearance, I'd seen it coming, but to hear him say it broke my heart. The old man loved his little place in the woods, had built it himself decades before I ever knew him, and had a right tidy place there. And all my fault for bringing Thomas and, in turn, his pursuers through there. "Is it gone, Jack?"

"I'm getting to that, don't rush a man when he's telling a story. My, but this is thirsty work." Jack looked around him, at our spare camp. "And me without a jug at hand. I tell you never was a man more distressed than I am when there ain't the comforts of a crock of the fire juice within reach."

He ran a knobby hand down his face and winced once more as he felt the damage there. "Where was I? Oh, yes, the fire. Well I heard them hooting like a passel of owls outside, apparently enjoying watching my cabin turn from log to flame. I yipped a few rounds of 'Help!' and shouted enough to color the experience for them, so they'd believe I perished in the fire.

"Pretty soon I saw flame myself, only from the inside, bright yellow and orange tongues chewing at my roof. And the smoke! I tell you it was like being curled up inside a cookstove. I knew I had to do something right quick. Then it come to me, the solution to my salvation. You know what I did right there in that burning hovel? I smiled, yes, sir, I smiled at those flames. Not for long, though, as I remembered I was tied up and could barely crawl around on my belly like a worm. I used my chin

89

and my knees and inched forward over by the wobbly old table. You know in my kitchen area by the back wall?

"Well, under that keg where I keep, or used to keep, my flour—you know, it's the same one you rattled your big mitts in that first night you come along in that blizzard like a big, half-naked grizz cub. You was trying to help me fix biscuits as I recall, only you weren't none too good at the task, I tell you. Back there, in the dirt, under a few layers of this and that, I have me a hidey-hole. But that ain't all. That hidey-hole leads to a tunnel."

He laid a finger alongside his nose again and nodded at me as if in conspiracy.

"A tunnel?" I said, my eyes widening despite my pain. "You never told me about that."

"You think I tell you everything about Maple Jack's life and times? Not a prayer, boy. You got to learn the facts as I dribble them out, and be glad of them." He winked. "Truth is I'd all but forgotten about it myself. It had been so long since I built it, and never have needed it, when it did come to me, it was as if placed in my head by the hand of the Almighty himself. Still, I feared the tunnel had long since collapsed in on itself."

"What did you build it for?"

"For the Sioux, of course," he said, shaking his head at my glaring ignorance. Of course, the Sioux.

"What about the Sioux, don't they use the door when they visit?" I knew that would rile him. He clucked like a flustered chicken, waved his arms and shook his frazzled head at me. That was the Jack I knew. Back to his old riled-up self.

"I dug it oh, twenty, thirty years back, when the Sioux had their breechclouts in a twist. They were on the warpath, raiding all over the land. I figured it was only a matter of time before they come upon me, trapping on their lands as I was. But they simmered down before I could put the tunnel to use.

"Before I could explore that old tunnel, I had to fetch that hatchet, cut off the ropes that bound me. But the smoke got so thick so quick, I knew time spent looking for the hatchet was too precious. I had to use my last moments in there to uncover my hidey-hole right quick, else I'd never live to find it. By then I was coughing enough to send a lung right up my windpipe."

"You found it, then?"

"What? My lung?"

Sometimes Jack can be thick.

"No, your hidey-hole."

"Course I did, how else you think I got here? I worry about you, Roamer." Jack shook his head. "You take one more knock to the bean and you ain't going to be worth much more than grizz bait. A whole heap of it, but still."

He tapped his temple and narrowed his eyes, as if trying to see into my own head. "Now where was I? Oh, yes, so I used my teeth and my face to drag away the dirt and knobby old logs I'd covered that hole with. It was dusty work, what with the smoke above me and the dirt in my face. I felt ready for a swig from the jug. And do you know, I had myself a jug in another hidey-hole elsewhere in the cabin, but it was too far away in the smoky dark to find.

"Of a sudden, I heard my roof timbers crackle and snap! And I knew it was but a matter of minutes, maybe seconds, before they fell in on me. I kept at it and soon enough I broke on through into that musty old dirt hole. And none too soon—that fire was hotting up right quick and too close to my raised backside for my comfort, I tell you. Then it commenced to burning my face, my head, and these buckskins. Oh, but I yearned for a swig from the whiskey jug."

"Not water?"

"No, no, never! Water don't do nothing in a situation like that. A man has to have whiskey, plain and simple.

"Oh, but that tunnel was filled to brimming with all manner of creeping slinkers, spiders, mostly, and their tangly leavings. Why don't they clean up after themselves, anyhow? The worst was that bull rattler, Leopold. You recall I told you about him? Well, that's where he lives. Never told you that, 'cause I didn't rightly know it myself. Not until I met up with him, that is. He keeps the rats and mice from populating my larder. But I reckon he figures he has full run of the tunnel, 'cause he set up a rattle-tail commotion like none I ever did hear in all my days. And me without a lamp or torch."

"What did you do?" I said.

"About what?"

Jack could be infuriating. "You know darn well about what—Leopold, the snake."

"Oh, him. Well, I had to creep forward like a legless coyote, dragging myself along by my chin hairs. When I reckoned I was out of striking range, I commenced to talking to that old, coiled bastard."

"Oh, so you bored him to sleep, eh?"

"What? You ungrateful whelp. I ought to . . ."

"Kidding, Jack."

"Okay, then. So I come to a truce with him. Remember now, it was all I could do to move along like a woolly worm, using my chin and my knees, sort of flopping my way along. By the time I got to old Leopold, he wasn't there. I reckon I talked him out of sinking fang on me that day."

"You think it might have been the smoke that got to him?" I said, goading him too much, perhaps.

"Smoke? Why don't you know nothing I've told you, boy? Snakes can't smell! Leastways not like you or me. Why, to them, smoke smells like day and night like water."

I had no idea what he was talking about and I've known Maple Jack long enough to know he likely didn't either. He talks sometimes to fill the air with words, especially when he didn't have a ready answer. With a little formal schooling the man might have made a prime poet or a politician.

I admit his story left me feeling better in some ways, though heartsick knowing I'd brought all this down on his poor, singed head. "Jack," I said. "How'd you get here? You walk?"

You would have thought I'd smacked him with a dead fish the way he recoiled and looked at me with a sneer. "Walk! Walk? Do I look like the sort of fella who'd walk, especially to save your mangy hide?" He poked the coals with a stick, then winked at me.

"Them rascals didn't know about the tunnel, see, and they sure as hell didn't know about the meadow. I had Ol' Mossback pastured up back. That's where the tunnel peeks out. I'd near forgotten where it might end up dumping me. I was more concerned with dragging myself along on my blasted face, smoke chasing me the entire way. I half thought flame would follow it, and visions of that tunnel turning into some sort of a sideways chimney kept me scootin' right along, I tell you, mister." He nodded as if agreeing with himself.

"I made it out all right, though. By then it was near dark, so I laid low, did my best to keep my sounds to an occasional low fart and belch, though I will allow as how I may have let a few curses fly. They sort of bubbled up and out before I could stop 'em. I was irate, I tell you. Plumb fit to be tied."

"You were tied, Jack."

"Yes, that's true. But not for long. See . . ." He grinned again and leaned close.

I think he almost enjoyed the entire awful escapade. Or at least the bits where he was able to triumph. The man will take pleasure in even the most minor victory.

"That whole time I spent trying to be quiet, and not looking downslope through the trees at my burning cabin, I sat sidled up to a jag of rock with enough edge on it to hack through those ropes. Wasn't but the work of an hour or so before I had one length cut through. Problem was it didn't do no good. No matter how I twisted and squirmed like a head-caught snake I couldn't loosen that wrap."

"What did you do?"

"I started in on another one. Took a spell but it was worth it, freed me up in no time. By then, of course, it was dark as a gravedigger's backside, and getting nippy, too. I was missing my bed, I tell you. All them skins soft as silk laid on me—and all burnt up. I hunkered down and pulled leaves over myself, managed to get an hour or two of shut-eye. I dreaded morning. I reckoned them that did it to me would be long gone—I would flee was I in their shoes. But what I was most fearful of was seeing my little cabin all caved in on itself.

"I knew it had disappeared in flame because before full dark I couldn't make out much of it from where I was holed-up above. I didn't dare prairie dog my head much as I didn't know if those rascals might have stayed.

"Come morning, I confirmed my suspicions. I stood, gave a good look-see, and that cabin was a black nub, all sunken like an old, toothless man's mouth. Took me a spell but I found Mossback, still grazing along the north edge of the meadow. I'd hobbled him, thinking I'd have gone back for him the day before. None of it seemed to bother him. He's yonder."

Jack nodded backward over his right shoulder and I could make out the distinctive mule's silvered snout and long perked ears. I'm sure he knew we'd been speaking of him.

"Steadfast and true, he is." I smiled, leaned back. "I don't suppose you know how badly I've been shot, do you?"

"Wondering when you were going to get around to asking."

"No sense interrupting a man with a story to tell. Especially one so riveting." I tried a smile, but I was fading.

"I won't mince my words, boy. You been shot up pretty good. Looks like a razor-hoofed horse from hell drove a foot right into that shoulder."

I looked down at my left shoulder, but all I could see was a charred Indian blanket.

"Done my best to doctor you. Got you packed up tight in there with a special comfrey poultice. It should draw out the badness as it seeps in. Rest of it, well, that's flesh and bone and ain't nothing can heal that but time, maybe with a nudge from the Good Lord."

"That your way of telling me I might not die?"

Jack's look was not one I was accustomed to seeing on his life-hard face. If I wasn't in such dizzy condition, I could almost swear he was tearing up, that lip—what I could see of it anyway beneath those burnt and puckered beard hairs—was all atremble.

"Die?" he said, his voice quiet, threatening to crack. "Why, no, boy. No, you ain't about to die off." He stood and squared his shoulders. "Maple Jack ain't lost a pard yet, and I don't believe today is looking like a day he's about to commence down that foul path. You get some rest. We're safe here for now."

"Jack, about Thomas. Do you think he's . . ."

"He's bound to be fine, for the same reason I give you before. He's a good boy, bit soft in the balls, but good-hearted. In my experience, such fools end up well. You don't worry about it. You can help him more by healing quick."

"I have to go after them."

"Smartest move is for us to head on back down out of these hills and get the law interested in these shenanigans."

"Can't do it, Jack." I shook my head and tried to rise, a wave of sudden cold crashed down on my head. I kept pushing, trying to work through it. "Have to go after them. I've had my fill of the law and it's never served me well."

Jack scuffed over to my side, eased me back down. It was then I saw my pillow was a gather of leaves with boughs laid over the top. We truly were stranded with nothing more than what was in our pockets.

"All of this palaver won't amount to a hill of farts if you don't heal up. You can't move nohow, so rest while I tend to supper."

Something about that struck me as odd. "What are we going to eat?"

"You never mind. Ol' Jack didn't come empty-handed to your little party. I rummaged in the ashes, managed to find a few items from the pile of black logs. Bits and bobs. It'll be enough."

I was feeling too weak and worked over to argue, but I wasn't worried. Maple Jack can survive anywhere, and likely thrive in this, his home environment. The man can catch fish with his bare hands—tickling he calls it. The technique really works, too. You lay on your belly alongside a creek or river, and gently ease your hands into the water. Then you work around under there, slow and steady, until you feel a fish.

You might think they would spook, but most of the time they don't, they stay right there. Then, and this will sound odd but it's the truth, you tickle them. Sort of run your fingertips up and down their bellies, slow and easy. The technique is one that takes a bit of practice—I fancy I've become adept at it. But no one can catch bankside trouts like Maple Jack.

And then there's snaring. I've been snaring rabbits and other edible critters for quite some time, but no method compares with Jack's. He can catch those bunnies all day long and end up with a full belly and enough soft skins for a coat.

We ended up staying in that cursed camp for three days. It about killed me to wait that long. I spent every waking second trying to prove to him I was getting better. I worked like a demon at it, knowing full well that if an infection were to set in, I might be a goner.

On the morning of the third day, I could take it no longer. I had to get up. I felt my muscles weaken with each passing minute, and I detest weakness. Suspecting my agitation, Jack surprised me with a stout cane, something he had hacked off and carved himself from the limb of a nearby ponderosa.

"I thought about what you said, and there is no sense heading back to get the law, the nearest being in Forsaken." Jack looked at me knowingly. "When the time comes, I will help load your big ass up onto Mossy. We'll plod along as best we can."

I had shared with him the thieving the lawdog there gave me. We were in agreement that folks who feed off others need to be stopped and punished in kind. But that was a worry for another time. We had to catch up with those three who'd done us wrong, and hopefully find Thomas alive.

I'd never forgive myself if he came to harm, though I knew it was not really my fault he was in his raw fix. If I had to lay blame elsewhere, I'd set it at the feet of that vicious creature called circumstance, always lurking in the shadowy corners at the far edges of life.

But I wouldn't do that, for to me that is another way of shifting blame. It's the action of people who give up, sit back, and let badness happen to them, over and over again. I never have been that way, and I wasn't about to, as Jack would say, "commence to be that person now."

"Jack, we only have one rideable critter between us. Those bastards took Tiny Boy with them. He's reason enough for me to go ahead and find them. Let alone Thomas. Even the girl deserves help."

"You have to be joshing me," said Jack. "She's in cahoots with them. Bah, you better get your hat on straight, son, because that little witch is up to no good. Matter of time before she's caught crouched over a bubbling cauldron, chanting incantations, and turning poor innocent folk into horny toads and lizards and mewling, half-formed beasts too awful for words!"

"Why, Jack, you are particularly vocal today. Might be you got a good night's sleep last night?"

"What if I did? Don't I deserve it?"

He stalked off, but I knew he was feeling good and was, for certain, no longer inclined to drag our sorry backsides toward Forsaken.

If anything could be done to those four thieving, burning cowards, it was up to me and Maple Jack to get it done. And we had already wasted too much time waiting for me to heal enough to travel.

"We need to leave."

"You need to rest up and heal," said Jack, rummaging in his meager stores. But I knew he was prepping to leave.

"In the morning, then?" I said.

"Yeah, I reckon. But it's foolhardy." He turned on me, pointing a steady finger, flint sparking in his eyes. "Don't let me hear you yelpin' and yammerin' about how sore you are. It ain't gonna be pretty."

CHAPTER TWELVE

The next morning we loaded up. Or rather I did. I tried my best to make Jack ride his mule, said I could walk alongside, that it would do me good to stretch my legs. But Jack is as knob-headed as Ol' Mossback. So there I was, blocked in on both sides by mulishness. Nothing I could do but mount up—with Jack's help.

I was as weak as a runt kitten and halfway up to the near-bare back of the mule when I thought how wrong I'd been and how right Jack was, once again. I should have stayed put at least another day or two. Hell, I could have used a month without flustering my blasted body and beaten head.

Almost from the start, he griped—Jack, not the mule—about how I was too big to be riding the mule, how I would likely collapse the beast to the ground under my bulk. Not what a fellow with a swimming head and a bullet wound wants to hear. Two days before it had been sewed up tight with hairs from the mule's tail. Jack used one of the needles he kept in the possibles bag always hanging around his neck.

It was slow going, and with each step I winced and did my best not to groan. It occurred to me, noting the irony, that I sounded like Thomas in that respect. I did my best to stifle my moans and wheezes, hot threads of pain pulsing in my wound, the cannon fire betwixt my ears smacking in counterpoint.

It took longer than it should have, but it finally dawned on me that Jack had been through his own hellish tortures at the rough hands and boots and torches of those would-be killers. He limped and winced and walked alongside the mule, each step a trial to him. It made me sick to see, for so many reasons.

"Jack, this is no good, we can't go on like this. You're as stoved up as I am and I can barely hang on to this poor mule."

Jack stopped, and as if reading his mind, Ol' Mossback stopped at the same time, looking forward, one ear flicked, waiting for our next decision with more patience than I have ever seen in a human.

My mentor turned a gray face up to me. To my surprise, he didn't argue. "I know, boy. But we have to gain some ground. We ain't been at this but a couple of hours. Let's give it at least another hour. That'll put us further along up the trail. Maybe we'll find some sign."

I nodded. "Then help me down, Jack. I can lean against Mossy. If you won't ride, at least it will give him a rest from hauling my carcass up and down these hills."

Jack smiled. "Must be his bony old hide is getting to your soft backside. He ain't nearly as padded out as that bug soft lummox you ride."

"Now see here," I said, preparing to swing my leg up and over the mule, "there's no need to work up a case against Tiny Boy when he isn't even here to defend himself."

Jack's a clever man. He got me talking and thinking about something else while I worked to slide down off the mule. It helped, though not as much as I would have liked. The motion felt like I had a handful of hot coals jammed down inside me. I said as much to Jack.

"What makes you think I didn't stuff a few heated-up river rocks in that teensy bullet hole before I sewed her up? You was caterwaulin' and carrying on so much you'd-a never noticed."

Jack didn't mount up, but after a few minutes of rest, we resumed our trek. I figure out a routine, tried to go it alone without leaning on Mossback for support, but that took too long. I moved about as fast as a porcupine climbs, that is to say . . . not at all fast.

In that stilted, dragging manner we made our way toward that day's sunset, working along the trail, following their sign— Tiny Boy's shoe prints alone were easy to follow, his Percheron hooves are massive. But it almost didn't matter, as those we pursued took no pains to hide their back trail, suspecting correctly in their minds that they had dispatched the only two people who had the potential to disrupt their plans, whatever they may be.

We tottered along in this fashion, hours more than I thought we could have—Jack's stamina knows no limits. To keep my mind from the lances of pain zigging through my chest, I concentrated on this foul undertaking from its beginning. I came up with lots of questions, few answers, and too many threads of speculation. None of it made sense, that was all I could come up with.

My fevered mind did return to one vision time after time, the face of that pretty but dastardly girl. Or was she? Her shouts and screams in defense of Thomas, of me, rattled in my aching head. Yet the way she threw herself at the man who'd shot me made little sense. Could she have been telling the truth? Why whisper in the dark, likely with the man who had shot me?

Somehow the more I thought about her, the more I felt certain she was, if not wholly intent on bad deeds, at least not responsible for how events progressed as they had.

The notions warred and balled up in my mind, and I decided I'd share them with Jack once we were seated at a fire. Maybe he could help me parse them.

"Roamer."

It was Jack, tugging gently on my sleeve. "Roamer, boy, we've stopped, reached the end of our tether for the night. Wake up or

I'll leave you standing here."

It was still early, not yet nightfall, but the air had grown colder. We'd made decent progress for two stoved-up men and an indulgent mule.

Jack foraged for late-season herbs and I did my best to rough out a fire spot and not fall over in a heap. I was still dizzy, though I fancy I had improved since the morning.

Jack packed a new hot poultice on my shoulder and muttered about how blazing red the wound was. He didn't like it and I wasn't too thrilled with it, either. That usually meant it was festering inside, and that often led to nothing good, a quick downhill trip with a sudden stop at the bottom—in the form of a hole six feet deep. Still, he kept on muttering and chewing leaves and heating them up and mashing them, and doing lord-knows what else, packing it all on there.

We made it an early night, I slept like a log and only awoke in full daylight to the sound of Jack fixing a scant breakfast for us. We spoke little, and resumed our trek.

Neither of us, I'm sure, had a slight notion of what we would do once we tracked down the bastards who did this to us.

Near the end of that second day, we found the girl.

CHAPTER THIRTEEN

We found Carla, the pretty girl whom Thomas doted on, who flatteringly, if falsely, pretended to be smitten with him, the same girl who'd toyed with me when I'd been gathering firewood, the one who'd brought Maple Jack's gentlemanly ways to bubble to the surface of his gruff old self.

We found her dead, off the trail, hanging stiff and still from the broad branch of an aspen.

Her neck was black-purple, her head canted too far to her left, her once-pretty face now sullied, the lips also blue-black, a thick wad of something stuffed in her mouth. It took me a few seconds before I realized it was her own swollen tongue, overflowing her mouth.

One eye was swollen and slitted, the eye itself barely visible peeking between as if accusing us of being too damn late to be of any use. The other eye had popped, bulging out but staring, thankfully, away, cast toward the trees as if considering them for the first time.

I've rarely seen Jack shaken. The man can keep his emotions tamped down. Says it helps him avoid dicey situations at the gambling tables. But when we saw the girl, we both whooshed out our breaths as if we'd been simultaneously driven hard in the guts by an unseen fist.

Her long, pretty red-and-white dress, one of two I'd seen her wearing, hung limp all about her. The bottom was soiled with dirt, evidence of having been dragged, perhaps. Her hands were

103

tied behind her back. There was evidence, too, that she had soiled herself in her throes of death, a common occurrence in a hanging. One of her boots lay on the ground, on its side beneath her. How hard she must have kicked to lose it from her foot.

After long silent moments, Jack shuffled over to where they'd tied off the rope around the tree's stout trunk. He struggled with the knot.

"Can't get it, blast it. It's too tight, and I don't have a knife, nothing to cut her down with. The bastards. The bastards." Still, through gritted teeth he worked his stubby, grimy fingers at the knot, gaining no headway.

Then I had a thought, a grim, horrible thought, but I followed it anyway. I walked over to the girl and paused a moment, then reached out toward the bottom of her dress.

"Boy, what are you doing?"

I turned red, tired eyes on Jack, then resumed my horrible little task. I reached up under her dress, felt along her leg, and was rewarded with the unyielding touch of stiff, cold flesh.

"Roamer!"

Jack came toward me and was about to shove me, wound or no, when with a tug, what I'd sought came free in my hand. I stepped back, held out the sheathed Bowie.

Jack stopped, stare at the knife, at me, rage still seaming his face, red boiling beneath the singed gray beard.

"A girl has to have protection out here in the West." It was all I could say. After a moment, when we stared at each other, I wagged the knife. "Cut her down," I said.

He reached out for the knife, hesitated, his fingers curling back on themselves, then took it from me gingerly. I followed him to the rope, grabbed the taut angle of it as he sliced, and held it so she wouldn't drop hard to the ground.

Jack is a good deal shorter than me, so I motioned to him to hold the rope. He read my intentions and lowered her as much as he could before he ran out of height. I scooped her with my good arm as best I could, easing her to the ground.

Jack put her boot back on and I checked two pockets on her dress for sign of anything that might tell us who she really was. I found nothing. We used a flat rock and the knife to dig up a grave close by the spot of her death.

We couldn't leave her unburied, the mountain critters would worry her corpse until it was nothing but dragged and scattered bones. I don't care if she was a pretty little devil in a dress, she was someone's daughter and had not been unkind to either of us.

The grave was shallower than it ought to have been, but the spot was boney with rock. We did our best to make her appear dignified, straightened her head, closed her eyelids, though in that we were largely unsuccessful, and folded her hands on her belly. We laid curls of aspen bark over her face so the dirt would not press in there, and then we covered her up. Scooping the soil in one dragged handful at a time.

Lastly we piled the grave long and well with rocks, and in this manner did our best to foil those who would dig her up and devour her.

At the end, we built a crude cross of branches, and Jack scavenged lengths of pliable root to secure it. I carved the name "Carla" on it, with her date of death, as near to the day as I could make it. Who knows? Perhaps she told the truth, at least in part, and her kin ranched not far from the spot. I would do my best to find out.

Later, over our grim little fire, I began to tell Jack how I knew about the girl's knife.

"I don't want to know," he said, his voice tight, cold, and clipped.

"But I want you to know." That seemed to settle it. I told him, quickly, quietly, and that was that. I'd not have Jack thinking I was some sort of philandering devil. I should have known better, but his opinion of me matters more than much else in my life.

"Well, the foulness of it aside," I said, "we know the vicious bastards we're dealing with are cruel beyond compare."

Jack nodded and sighed. "As my old pappy used to say, 'You sleep with hounds, you wake up with fleas.' I reckon she knew what sort she was dallying with when she teamed up with those who did this to her."

"I doubt she expected to end up like this. She tried to stop the man from shooting me."

"See now, she was a good girl when it counted. That's what we got to believe, Roamer."

All I could do was nod. My throat lumped up once more. "I know it," I finally managed to say.

"Let's get some sleep so we can track the beasts who did this. I have a powerful urge to kill them right back for what they've done here."

I nodded, in complete agreement.

CHAPTER FOURTEEN

We lit out early the next morning.

Jack fired a question at me that surprised me. "What do you think of the notion that your man Thomas is one of them?"

"One of who?" I said, knowing what he was referring to. "You don't mean to say he's in league with the bad apples we're tracking."

Jack shrugged. "It's a thought. It ain't like he's given you cause to think otherwise."

"We don't even know what it is he's really after, nor them."

"We know about the deed, odd as it is. But that's all."

"Well, it's pretty obvious to me they want the property, or something about it—timber rights, minerals, who knows?"

"Mm-hmm," said Jack, not really buying what I was selling, I could tell. And so it went, with us confabulating, as Jack likes to call it, back and forth, slow and steady, hour after hour.

We kept up our chatter like two foolish birds. It was a feeble effort to fill the air and our thoughts with anything other than the memory of finding the girl as we had. I can safely say we were both disturbed and angry over her death. Somehow, I felt guilty about it, too.

It was long past the noon hour, and all we had between us were a few handfuls of cornmeal and whatever else Jack had managed to scavenge along the trail—we had no time to set snare for rabbit, and as we had no guns we could bring down no game. The girl's knife, a useful tool, still carried with it a spooky feeling, though not enough to prevent us from using it.

As I said, past the midday hour we rested a bit, then resumed our shambling procession up the trail. We were both afoot, as it was far too much work for me to climb on and off the poor mule. Ol' Mossback is a stout creature, but he's no Tiny Boy. I had enough to feel guilty over, I didn't want to add killing Jack's mule to the list.

We'd given up on chatter, as neither of us wanted to voice the notion that we were accomplishing next to nothing. Then, rising from the nearest hill in the trail, there appeared before us the outline of a man's head, then shoulders, swaying side to side as if riding.

We both saw him at the same time. Jack held out a hand before my belly to stop me. Even the mule stood stock-still, ears perked toward the approaching rider.

The rest of the man slowly emerged from the rise. He was lit by the sun, and we could not make out his face. But there was something about him that seemed familiar. Wishful thinking, I told myself.

"Who do you suppose . . . ?" said Jack in a low voice.

"No idea, but by now he's seen us as sure as we've seen him."

"Then let's hold up here and see what the man has to offer." It was an obvious response since we were in a mostly treeless stretch, all waving brown grasses and few boulders. The visible rocks and trees were too far off the trail for a pair of slowpokes to make for.

"You got that walking stick I made you?" said Jack, not taking his eyes from the man.

"Yep, and you have the knife," I replied.

"Yep."

We didn't have long to wait. As soon as a skidding cloudbank dragged itself before the sun, light shone on his face and I saw the man for who he was—the horse-faced brute who'd shot me, who'd been in on setting Jack's house afire, who trussed Jack, and who seemed the likely culprit to have strung up the girl.

He didn't slow his horse's pace a whit, even when the horse perked its ears forward at the sight of Mossy. We waited. From two dozen yards away I saw recognition draw a wide smile on his face. He straightened his shoulders, sat up, and parted his coat with his hands. No doubt to snatch at his weapons, one of which was Maple Jack's old war cannon.

"You recognize him, don't you?" I said.

Jack nodded. We waited, watching him advance in no hurry.

"Well now," said the man, reining up a dozen yards from us.

Yep, it was indeed the long-faced bastard, his big teeth gleaming as he all but brayed to us across the distance of the trail separating us. We said nothing.

"I have made it through a fair number of years without seeing a spook, so you will forgive me if I seem amazed at the sight of you two gentlemen!"

He let this attempt at levity hang in the air. Neither of us spoke. This wiped the stupid grin off his face. He gigged the horse a few steps closer, then stopped once more.

"Well now," he said, again, pausing for response. Receiving none he smiled once more. "Judging from the bloody mess your shoulder's wearing"—he nodded at me—"and the burnt cinder that used to be your head, old man"—he nodded at Jack—"I'd say you ain't ghosts. Just men who have had more than their share of luck."

He nudged his horse ahead a few more steps. It was a fine-looking bay. "Can't say as I'm surprised to see you. Had me a pricklin' of the neck, if you know what I mean. Felt like I had somebody lurking over my shoulder. Told the others I'd catch 'em up. In truth, I wanted me a taste of that little crumpet I expect you found back yonder. And now I can't find that harlot's

109

horse nowheres. Say, you all ain't seen it, have ya?"

The horse stepped forward once more.

I glanced quickly at Jack, saw his seared whiskers pulsing, knew he was gritting his teeth, his jaw muscles bunched tight.

"That's far enough," growled Jack.

That brought the man's smile up short, for a brief moment. "Surely you can't be serious, old man." He kept the horse walking. "A blind man could see you are unarmed, and so is that bloody bear next to you."

My mind stuttered over the possibilities open to us—damn few of them. I tightened my grip around the end of the stout stick of a cane Jack had made for me.

Horse Face made his play and gave us our one and only opening by being so cocksure and belligerent. He rode that horse right up to within two or three yards of us, at the same time shucking a revolver. It wasn't Jack's gun, that much was plain, which was even worse, for it would be quicker to shoot.

He raised it to chest height, but kept his eyes on Maple Jack, and I knew, in a fingersnap, that he was going to shoot Jack first. Right about then, Jack's knobby old hand whipped upward, the girl's knife clutched tight. He'd never make it in time.

I shoved Jack hard on the shoulder. He's a stout fellow, but didn't expect anything of the sort from me, so he pitched to the side, nearly off the trail. Mossy fidgeted nearby. At the same time I lashed out with my stout walking stick, more suited for use as a length of firewood, and smacked Mossback hard on the rump.

That mule seemed to know what was required of him because he dove head down, ears back, closed that gap between him and the horse, and barreled straight into the bay.

The horse had no time to think, no time to do much but rear up, a raw whinny boiling out of its throat. But Ol' Mossy gave it no chance to finish that cry of terror, for he caught the horse with both its front legs up off the earth, and kept on ramming. That crazy mule rammed his stout body into the horse like a locomotive.

The rider, Horse Face, shouted nonsense words and strangled cries as he tried to keep himself in the saddle, one hand flailing for the saddle horn, the other waving his revolver. He managed to crank off one shot that menaced nothing more than the treetops. His head snapped to and fro as if tethered to his body by a thread of yarn.

The mule plowed ahead as if the horse wasn't there. I have no idea what made him go berserk like that—I didn't smack him on the backside that hard—but figured Jack would feed me an elaborate amount of reasoning later. If we could deal with this killer as we hoped.

As soon as the mule barreled into action, I lumbered forward, as did Jack, flanking the flailing mass of mule, horse, and man. We only had scant seconds before he either dismounted or leveled off a shot at one of us. I grabbed at the bay's sagged, jouncing reins as much to steady myself, but the horse danced too fast and I let go, staggering.

I saw the top of Jack's head across the horse's withers, saw a sneer on his blistered, seared face. His arm rose up in an arc, the girl's knife's handle gripped in his hand, the blade driving hard at the side of the horse.

What's he doing? I thought, but knowing better than to doubt the man. He could no more harm a horse than would I. As if time had slowed, Jack's arm rose up and down, up and down. Each yank back revealed a blade slick with strings of raw-red blood. Still he aimed a following blow straight at the horse. Then I realized what Jack was up to—stabbing the man. Blind, raw rage had taken over.

I took my cue from Jack and regaining my balance, swung that stout walking stick like a club, hard as I could, straight at the bastardly rider's midsection.

One or both of us were successful, for the man's screams clawed their way from his throat, one ripping over the next as if fighting their way up and out of his mouth. My stick slammed his ribcage, drove in neatly beneath his flailing raised left arm, and rammed hard and direct as you please before it snapped apart.

I am certain much of the cracking, splintering I felt was not just the stick, but the man's ribs. I saw the side of him cave in. I relished the feeling and gave that long-faced bastard another and another, until I had no useable length of stick with which to thrash him.

The killer's revolver had spun from his grasp and landed somewhere in the dirt. He was in too much pain to grab for another weapon. The horse had grown far too rambunctious, churning and stomping in place, its teeth a blur of white, rolling eyes matching, head thrashing side to side, foamy spittle spraying.

As the horse crowhopped forward a half dozen paces, we stepped away at about the same time. I saw Jack across from me, his chest rising and falling hard, his gray-black hair every which way, wilder than usual, his bruised face set in a mask of raw rage, teeth gritted, and spattered with blood from the man's leg where Jack's frantic lunges had stabbed and stabbed.

The killer, jerking atop the wild horse like a rat shaken by a terrier, pitched to his left, his right boot stuck in the stirrup. A gray wool sock dangled from the tip of a long, bony, white foot at the end of a long, raised right leg. I watched as he pivoted up and over, blood spouting from a half dozen punctures in his thigh and lower gut. He screamed and screamed and kept right on screaming until, with his left foot still in the stirrup, he hit the ground hard.

I watched his head slam, carom off the hard-packed earth. As the horse danced forward, the killer's body and head lurched straight under that horse. A big rear hoof stomped down hard on the man's battered head. Something popped, and the boot came out of the stirrup. It was twisted and the toes pointed in the opposite direction they should be.

It didn't matter, the man was far beyond being able to walk. I hobbled over as the horse, belly heaving and head whipping, trotted off down the side of the trail. For all that, the man's chest convulsed with hard-drawn, ragged breaths. I smelled too much at once—horse shit and man shit and blood and gunsmoke, and above it all, the one thing we all shared, men and beasts alike, the stink of fear. This situation was unexpected and awful and reeked to high heaven.

But it got the job done.

Jack and I stared down at him as his breaths lessened. Finally he pulled in a great rush of air, held it longer than possible, then it leaked out in a last slow sigh.

We neither of us spoke for a full minute, then Jack straightened, rubbed his right shoulder, about where I'd shoved him to get him out of the line of fire. "Thanks, by the way. Saved my hide. I reckon we're even."

"Somehow I doubt that," I said, hoping to smile him or rile him, I didn't much care which. Jack wore a dark look I'd rarely seen on his face. Past experience told me it was a tough one to shake loose once it settled in.

He stuffed the knife in the sheath, and flexed his hand, still staring down at the man. "I'd piss on him if I could, but I think I already wet myself in the fracas." He turned and ambled off trail after the horse.

I toed the man's bent boot. I've been surprised more than once by a critter playing dead—more often than not the two-legged sort. Convinced he was as dead as he was going to get, I bent, grunted, and grabbed a bunch of his trouser leg in a fist. I dragged him off the trail, over on the high side, laid him out close by a low snarl of rabbit brush.

I'd finished going through his pockets and unstrapping his gun belt when I heard a shout. I grabbed the remaining revolver, Jack's brute of a weapon, and spun.

"Luck of luck, boy!" It was Jack shouting to me from off the trail.

I stood, holding the gun. There came Jack, leading the killer's horse, saddle, supplies, and all. My stomach growled louder than a boar grizz in April.

"I heard that," said Jack, smiling. "Reckon he has more than measly cornmeal in these bags, eh?"

Just then, Mossback the mule came plodding back down the trail. He looked anywhere but at us, one big ear twitching like a leaf in a stiff breeze.

"I don't know whether to thank you or give you a lickin', you crazy-headed critter!" Even as he said it Jack smiled. The mule walked up to within ten feet of him and stood, still not looking at either of us.

"Let's keep him and that horse apart for now," said Jack. "Mossy might be docile until he ain't, but this horse is wound tighter than a fiddle string at a liquored-up hoedown."

"How did you catch it?"

"What do you mean, how did I catch it? I took off after it. I am a swift runner, I will have you know."

I stared him down.

He turned, mumbled, "Reins fetched up on a jaggedy old stump. Another second and I'd have had to bid him adios."

"Well, at least you were fast enough for that." I smiled at his weak attempt to look ornery. "This is one mule I will never cross," I said, walking over to Ol' Mossy. I lashed his reins to a low pine snag and made my way back to Jack and the horse.

The horse was a jumpy beast with wide eyes and a body all

atremble. Blood streaked its heaving right side. The saddle and the lashed-down bundles behind the cantle were hanging askew, but they were all there.

I wound the reins around a low jut of rock for leverage and did my best to cluck and offer soothing sounds while Jack chased the beast in a tight circle, loosening the cinch and straps as they danced. It eventually worked and the whole apparatus flopped to the ground. If the horse decided to bolt, at least now we had gear. Next order of business was to hobble and tie her securely to something.

We sorted through the man's gear and found a surprising amount of useful items, a good many of them familiar to Jack. Horse Face's traps sported a fine assortment of food, coffee, and spices. Jack wanted to move on then and there, and went so far as to begin repacking the man's bags. I, on the other hand, wanted to stay put, make some grub and hot coffee. I am partial to a cup of hot coffee most any time of the day or night.

I sighed and turned my attention to hauling rocks around the body.

"Why you wanna go and do that? And for him? You already laid him out nice and straight. Ain't no one but his mama would care, and she ain't around. And even if she was, she'd like as not curse him and spit on his foul stove-in face anyhow!"

"It's not for him, Jack, it's for us. If we take pains to bury the bastard, then mark a stone with the word 'killer' or some such, maybe it will go easier on us when the law finds him. Hell, I don't know, I'm only trying to make whatever sense I can out of this mess. I don't think right when I've been addled and deprived of coffee."

Jack stared me down, finally nodded, and unpacked the coffee. He kindled a little flame and we made a couple of precious cups' worth, then sampled more of the man's jerky. Elk, I think, and damn tasty.

Refreshed and invigorated—as much as two busted-up rigs like us could feel, anyway—we covered the horse-faced bastard with rocks. We agreed there was no point in digging a hole for him first. He wasn't worth the time and we didn't want to make it too difficult for the critters. Just enough to ease my own conscience. Jack wasn't burdened with such where this weasel was concerned.

I topped the misshapen rocky mound with a flat rock on which I scratched: "Murderer."

I had little inclination to write more, nor further information to aid me in the task. We packed up once more, saddled the horse, and made ready to go.

"Makes sense you should ride Mossy. This horse is still fidgety, but not nearly big enough to hold that body of yours up."

I couldn't disagree, but I'd be lying if I said it doesn't sting when people point out the obvious about my size. Double that with the fact that I'll never be mistaken for a dashing stage actor and you find me chewing my lip half the time, biting back the urge to lay into folks who usually don't know they've caused me annoyance. I can be thin-skinned and hardheaded.

It took a fair few minutes for Jack to keep that flighty bay upright and moving forward. It danced a jig when Jack hoisted his portly little body up and managed to keep his left foot in the stirrup. He clung to the saddle horn and bouncing like a poorly loaded pannier about to come undone. The only difference was this pannier howled and cursed and tried to shake a fist, all the while the bay churned the trail in good shape.

Eventually Jack got his right leg up and over and sawed those reins until the horse settled down. I was glad it was Jack on that jittery mount. I had begun to not see double, and all that commotion would surely have opened up my wound more than it did when we laid into that killer.

As for me, the mule gave no sign of ill content. Jack saw it, too, and harrumphed as if I were the cause of the horse's fidgety behavior. It was agreed I would ride ahead so the horse wouldn't travel in fear of the frightening beast behind it.

Before I mounted, I spent a good five minutes in the pucker-brush rummaging for Horse Face's revolver. I thought I'd seen it land when he'd lost hold of it. Turns out I was off the mark by a dozen feet.

Jack was only too glad to have his Dragoon back in hand and caressed it enough so I had to look away. He stuffed it into his waist sash, and thus armed, along with the newly acquired booted rifle on his saddle, we rode forward. Once we got on the trail, the day brightened, matching our rising spirits, and we decided to begin making up for the days of time we lost. Worry drove me. Revenge drove Jack.

CHAPTER FIFTEEN

The day's events had worked the zest out of the bay, for by afternoon she'd begun to poke along. Jack dug his moccasin heels in a time or two, but after a dozen such thumpings she failed to respond with much more than a quick step.

"Time to call it a day, Jack," I said, stopping and tugging Mossback into a half turn in the trail. A gust of wind hunched my shoulders, and that in turn made me wince. The shoulder was a tender mess, but I was pleased I was alive. Could have been a whole lot worse.

Jack's old popper might be big and intimidating and make a hellacious smoking stink and roar when it's fired, but the load in that bullet Horse Face plugged me with wasn't particularly powerful. It took a generous bite out of me, punched on through below my collarbone, chewing a hole big around as a double eagle, and lodged in there, at least until Jack fished it out some time before I first came around. Despite all that, it didn't kill me. But it did leave me weak as a wormy dog.

Jack took pity on me—not that I was looking for it, mind you. A man who seeks pity is no man. He's a weak-kneed rascal who'll turn tail if given the chance. That brought Thomas to mind. But more about that later.

"Yeah, this bay's about played out. I doubt even sidling up close to Mossy will give her much of a spookin', frazzled as she is." Jack managed to get her a few yards closer. "But that doesn't mean we should picket 'em close to one another. That mule, he's liable to take another fit and lay into this beast." Jack smiled, the first time in many hours.

We ranged ahead another quarter mile or so and managed to find a clearing on the right side of the trail where someone not too many days before had set up camp. A fire had been built tight below a flat-face boulder, a tumbledown from the rocky crags looming above us to our east.

That night I knew we would both eat well, at least compared with how we'd been dining. The man had had two wool blankets packed with clothes and rolled tight behind the saddle. I was looking forward to wrapping one of those blankets around me and sawing logs. The other blanket I recognized, and pointed it out to Jack.

"Yep," he said, eyeing the cloth. "That there's my decent old Hudson I have laid beneath many a night." He paused, looking upward in reverie as the setting sun washed the high rocks to the east. Soon the sky shone with soft light the color of a fresh egg yolk popping in the skillet.

"Not alone, I take it from your musing."

He spun on me, an accusing finger poised. If it had been a dagger, I'd be nursing a second wound. "Ain't no call to be rude, mister. Women, as a rule, are fair creatures and only no-accounts mock their beauty."

"I did nothing of the sort, Jack, and you know it. We're both too crabby to natter on right now. How about we break out that coffee?"

He nodded, knowing I was right. "Good, yes, that's the idea. And what's more, I do believe the man left us a bottle of sippin' whiskey."

We set up camp, benefactors of the logs someone had already dragged into place to either side of the fire spot. Then we availed ourselves of the remaining firewood the previous party had gathered. In no time we had the horse and mule settled, watered, and fed, their quiet munching sounds soothing in the day's waning light.

Jack managed to whip up a batch of johnnycake from cornmeal in the man's bag. Fried alongside them was a goodly share of thick slices of bacon carved from a muslin-wrapped slab, also from the man's stores. The sweet, smoky meat smelled too good for words and I seriously considered peeling that bacon right out of the pan and eating it half-cooked.

All in all, ridding the world of that killer and putting his food stocks to good use helped take the corroded edge off the fact that we had taken a man's life, or at least caused it to happen, even if it had been a matter of self-defense.

I tended the fire and readied the coffee. We had topped up our canteens twice along the way that day—and slaked our thirst at the same time. The horse and the mule had done the same.

"It's plain we're on their trail, and likely this was their camp," I said, wiping my mouth as demurely as I could on my buckskin shirt's grimy cuff. "I've told you my thoughts, but what do you reckon their motives are?"

"Well, as you say, it's that ranch deed, ain't it? I was a betting man and had the facts we do, that'd be my wager."

I nodded in agreement. "I keep mulling this over and can't parse any answers."

Jack shrugged, poured a liberal dose of whiskey in his coffee. "Maybe there ain't any."

"What if Thomas has already become useless to them? Seems logical if we assume the deed is what they're after."

Jack blew across the top of his tin cup. I kept quiet, knowing he was giving it thought, too. I welcomed his notions. He might be a hardscrabble sort, but the man's mind is sharp as a honed scythe.

"It don't make no sense, though, does it?" He eyed me over

the crackling little fire. "Just a deed? Got to be more to it than that. Course, if it was only the deed they was after, why keep him around? That Thomas is a squirly sort, and not likely good for much. As far as I can tell the man is useless. What good would he be to them?"

I must have pulled a pained face, because Jack set down his cup.

"What's wrong, boy? That wound open again? I can make a poultice."

"No, keep your seat, Jack. I'm fine. Relatively speaking, anyway."

"Oh, ho, there you go with your highfalutin' lingo again, I guess you're healing."

I had to chuckle at that. If anything, Jack uses more two-dollar words—or at least tries to—than any man I've ever met. But if I toss one in now and again, you can be sure he'll pounce on it like a cur on a meat scrap.

"I hope we aren't too late."

"Too late for what? To save that whelp? We'll do what we can, but hang fire, why are you so worried about him, anyway? Brother or no, it ain't like you owe him. Why, from what you told me the whole clan has done little more than scrub the bottoms of their boots on you!"

I fidgeted, I hemmed, and I hawed. And I couldn't think of a reason to disagree.

Jack leaned forward and squinted like he does when he has something important to say. "Even with all that, you've a soft spot for him, eh?"

"I guess I do." My tone was one of defeat, a hoarse croak.

"Good. That's one of the reasons I like you, Roamer. Got goodness in your heart. Too many of us mountain folk who come out here by nature and inclination—how's that for a word?—we sort of dry up inside, forget that just because we want to leave something behind don't mean we can. Nor should we."

He said that last with a few wags of his empty cup, for emphasis.

"I been thinkin' on this, boy, and I know we touched on it back when you all were at my place, but . . ."

I knew what he was about to say and leaned my head to one side. He took my meaning, but Maple Jack is nothing if not persistent.

"Now, now, hear me out. Humor an old man, will you?"

He took his time pouring another cup. The night had turned off chill and I held out my own cup, the sight of that steaming black liquid too tempting to pass up. When they were filled, and suitably topped with drizzles of whiskey, he resumed his chatter.

"As he's younger than you, that makes you the eldest. The rightful—"

I sighed and shook my head, but he plowed onward.

"Heir."

I had plenty of answers but none I had the strength to defend—always a concern when "confabulating" with Jack.

"Surely you want your share? A share of what's yours by birthright?"

I held up a big hand. "No, no I don't. I disowned them As far as everyone is concerned, me included, I never lived and Thomas is the rightful heir."

Jack recoiled as if I'd slapped him. "Now your talkin' loco! Never lived?"

"Not in their eyes, not in their world. They're better off without me and I am certainly better off without them."

"Then why are you so concerned about that greenhorn boy?"

I still had no good answer, save for a weak shrug. The shoulder protested with a stab of hot pain. We were quiet. Not far from the fire's ring I heard the padding and rustling of soft feet, low, numerous. Wolves maybe, likely coyotes.

Harmless, especially in the fall of a plentiful year. We'd come off a robust summer of good rains, and so, fat rodents and fatter predators. They'd go into the winter well fed instead of lean and slavering, a sight I'd seen often enough. More often in humans, though.

"Look, Jack. I have everything I want. Mostly to be shed of them. At least I thought I had that. But now that he's dropped himself in the midst of my life, and made a mess of it and of yours, too, I have to wrestle with it. Besides"—I pulled the blanket tighter around my shoulders, pinching at the throat—"they took my horse, my gear, and my books."

Jack nodded, smacked his hands on his knees. "And my lynx hat, the primal bastards!" He stood, knees popping in protest, and ambled off to wet a bush. Over his shoulder he said, "We'd best get a few hours of snorin' in and done. I'll take first watch."

I stood and tossed the last of my coffee on the fire. "All the same to you, Jack, I'll sit up first."

He came back, eyebrows pulled tight, but nodded.

I was worked up and figured I'd use the time to puzzle out this un-puzzle-able mess. As I leaned against a close-by knob of granite, it occurred to me I was once again overthinking the situation. It is a trait Jack has accused me of, rightfully, a number of times in the past. It appears I am slow to learn.

The bald facts were plain: The two remaining crooks had absconded with a greenhorn, intent on thieving something of value from him. Along the way they stole from me and from my best friend, then left us to die. A third number of their ilk killed a fourth number of their ilk, then we did for him. They had to be made to pay, one way or another.

I blew out a plume of frosty breath, barely visible in the dark. I had decided nothing, but knew if we dogged on, all would become clear in time. Tomorrow could not come soon enough.

Chapter Sixteen

I admit I spent my time on watch only half paying attention to the sounds and smells of the night around me. Something told me all we had to fear were our own overactive imaginations, and by that I meant my own. Thomas and his captors were far ahead, and likely thinking they were shed of us. And why wouldn't they?

It was Thomas I thought of as I did my best to keep from cramping up. It was early in the nippy season, but I already missed the warmth of a July evening in high country.

If he was still alive, Thomas was in need of someone to guide him, some figure to help point him in the right directions, down paths that would lead to fruitful undertakings and not criminal endeavors—or worse. He certainly didn't get it from the woman who had birthed us. And he damned sure didn't get it from our father.

That man was born to filch women's hearts, their jewels, and then their family fortunes. Why else had a lowborn member of Italian aristocracy been shunted off to America, no contact ever having been initiated with his own family back in his homeland?

Only one reason was plausible, only one was possible, knowing what I did of the man. He had run for his life, likely chased. (How many half siblings do I have in the world?) Too bad whoever he had wronged hadn't had the nerve or wherewithal to complete the task and kill him before he infected yet another bevy of hopeless souls on these shores.

At least in the case of my own mother, and I use the term in the most tenuous, threadlike connection imaginable, the reason for his attraction to her was obvious. She came from money. As old as old money could be in the United States, anyway. Her father's father had done everything a good Southern gentleman ought so he might amass his fortune, building up a sprawling cotton plantation on the backs and bellies, weary feet, hands, and souls of slaves, which he also bought and sold for much profit.

By the time dear old Papa came along, the family's status as a well-heeled nest of money-grubbing gentry was lodged firm and unmoving in the hard-packed Southern soil.

Yet who would have thought that a single, handsome, dashing, chivalrous-seeming Italian with a dubious pedigree and a hunger for finery, a thirst for good wine, and a lust for pretty women, namely the singular and perky young nose-in-the-air offspring of the Old General himself, could bring the entire affair to a penniless, screeching stop?

The hours of my watch passed slowly and yet I let Jack sleep on. I was in no mood to wake him. The man, no matter his bluster, is much older than I, though how old, I know not.

I wished to keep to myself for a few more minutes. I had dug far too deep into my own past, something I had not allowed myself to do in many years. I found it a painful task but one that somehow needed doing.

Thomas, once more in my life, unbidden and unwanted as he was there, had done this to me. I owed it to myself to sort out my intentions regarding the young fool well before I found him. Despite my enmity toward him, there was the fact that he was my brother, bloodwise the single person on earth I was closest to.

Thus I spent my night, in the dark, vaguely aware of various scurryings and scratchings and sliding sounds only ever heard in the dark by creatures whose lives are lived while others slept. I realized I could not truly discount my feelings for the boy.

Unearthing a reservoir of reluctance I had spent years covering over, I could not say with any amount of finality I did not wish to know him. That I did not wish to spend my life without staying in contact with him. I felt that way much of the time, but while there was still a sliver of uncertainty, I had to explore it. I had to make certain I was better off as the loner known as Roamer. A knight without a cause, questing for . . . what? Nothing?

All of this thinking might well be moot should we come upon them too late. There was every reason to think those two thieves had already killed Thomas. The thought tightened in my gut like a cold fist of stone. We had to make it to this fabled, deeded ranch soon. How far was it? I had no idea, only a vague memory of a vague map in my mind, what little I recalled from my brief glimpses at Thomas's fancy papers.

Lack of sleep can cause a man to think all manner of odd thoughts. And that night I was no exception. I roused from a light doze some time later by Jack's curses and growls. He is prone to being surly of a morning, and his efforts on that predawn day were doubled and directed at me for letting him sleep the night through. It must have done him good for he was in rare, fiery form.

"Were you a preacher in a former life, Jack?" I said, stretching and easing mobility into my stiff, cold joints. Oddly enough I felt pretty good for someone who had slept but half the night, and that half leaned against a cold boulder.

"What if we'd been attacked in the night? Eh? You . . . whelp!" He stomped off toward his favorite bush, grumbling the entire time.

I took pity on him and tried not to smirk while I stirred up the ashes and got a pot of coffee bubbling. By the time day's light fingered its way over the Bitterroots to our right, we were loading the last of the gear onto our rested steeds. To our relief, the bay was a calmer animal that day.

"I rode the starch out of her," said Jack, nodding in approval of himself, even though I doubted he'd had much do with it. It was decided I would continue to ride the mule and Jack the bay.

"In case she decides to kick up a fuss again," said Jack.

CHAPTER SEVENTEEN

We came upon the ranch later the following day. Save for an unidentifiable feeling of something about to happen—that neck-prickling sensation common to most folks at one time or another—the day had been uneventful. Then it all changed.

The trail we followed skinnied to little more than a footpath winding between fallen trees, copses of living trees, and all manner of tumbledown boulders. They were remnants of mighty earthly upheavals from long ago. A vague concern skittering along the edges of my mind began to present itself.

"Jack, how do you suppose the ranches we know to exist up north here in the Pascal Valley region get their goods?"

"Why, that road up north, yonder through the mountain pass would be one way, though it is treacherous in winter."

"Or damn near impassable."

"Yeah, but that route is handsome." Jack shook his head, smiling at the picture in his mind. "You take that trail through Pend d'Oreille land, you got yourself some pretty scenery."

"Yep, it's been a while since I've been through there. Strikes me it'd be a good way to cut on over to Montana then strike north to Salish Lake."

"Yep. Course I reckon the ranchers would do most of their traveling and trading to the west, over Walla Walla way."

I glanced at Jack. He rubbed his chin, raking his fingers through his oddly trimmed beard. He'd done his best to cut out the singed bits, but he wasn't too interested in his looks, at least not until he was set to visit with his "winter woman," as he called her. For now, he didn't seem to care that his beard and hair were a lopsided affair all around.

"But what you're wondering about, I'll bet, is the same notion I been cogitatin' on—this here trail ain't amountin' to a piss hole in the snow. That means we're likely coming in through the back door, so to speak. We keep on like this and we'll run out of trail before we run out of words to describe how poor it is."

As he spoke, still riding behind me a few yards, we reached the top of a rise and rounded a boulder that looked to be as big as Jack's old cabin. There was barely enough room for us to walk by.

I was set to dismount when I held up a hand. "Trail's ended, Jack," I said in a low voice.

"Well now, how do you like them apples?"

He was prepared to launch into a full-bore tirade of words, I am sure of it, but I shushed him. I'd have to explain the shushing pretty quickly or he'd get riled over that, too. Jack was in a touchy mood that day. Most days, if truth be told.

I lowered myself until I stood on the ground, and laid a hand on the mule's side to keep him from fidgeting. It's not a big concern with Mossback, but it doesn't pay to take chances when a man saw what I'd seen. I beckoned Jack with a finger. He judged that we needed to be quiet.

He led the horse forward, tied her off to a ponderosa close by the path, and walked up, trying to see around me. Not an easy task.

"What's cookin'?"

I stepped aside. "Take a peek."

He did and his eyebrows rose as expected. "No kidding. That the place?"

"I can't be certain. Might be a different one. You know there are quite a few ranches tucked away in river valleys over this way."

"We might as well approach." Jack didn't lift his eyes from the place, but kept whispering. "But if it is the one, we can't just up and ride on in and expect them to serve up tea and fancy cakes. We'd better do it quiet-like, no fuss."

"And if it isn't Thomas's ranch?"

"Then no harm done. We'll say we're weary rovers who got ourselves lost, maybe ask a few questions."

We'd been looking down the trail toward a perfect-looking little valley, a scattering of ranch buildings and corrals. I saw no sign of cattle, nor of humans. Something told me it was the place. "Abandoned?"

Jack grunted and continued eyeballing the scene. "Nope," he said, nodding toward the ranch house, up by the tree line.

Now I saw it, too. Gray smoke wisping from the chimney.

The house itself was a tidy, skinned-log affair with a long, low porch. We angled further around the rock and I saw four glass windows along the front of the house, two on the side. They all leached an oil lamp's low, warm glow outward into the darkening afternoon.

Genuine glass windows are a rarity out here, though from the looks of this place, it appeared whoever had built it were not concerned with money. The house was backed up to a dense, darkening forest of pine that marched up the sloping foothills that led to higher peaks far above and beyond.

In the meadow below the house a whole lot of care had been taken to construct chutes and gates, and I counted four corrals. They hadn't been used this season, though. Nothing sadder than a property that has spent seasons unused. Nature doesn't much care, it continues on sprouting thin, tall grasses where the corrals and lanes would have been pounded to dust from stomping, milling hooves of horses and beeves.

The place looked well built, perhaps had been there a decade or more. So how did Thomas's father, ahem, come by the property?

"Hey, Roamer." Jack nudged my arm. "We best figure out a plan. If tonight's the night, then I need food and coffee, not in that order. We best find a place to hide these critters, too."

"You get a fire going back along the trail a ways behind those rocks, that way they won't see it. We have to get down there and scout."

"You gone squirly in the head? All them windows in that fancy log shack, they'd spy us coming, going, and in between."

I wasn't sure what that meant, but he was right. "I'm worried about Thomas."

"Me, too, Roamer, but you go blustering on in there in daylight and they'll pick you off, sure as winter's cold, and where will the kid be then? And don't think I'm going to hotfoot it across that pasture and yarn your hide back to safety. No, sir."

"What's the plan, then?" I said, doing my best to remain rational. Not always an easy task for me.

"Like I said, we have some grub, coffee, maybe a little shut-eye. Then when it's dark, we wind on down there. We stick to the edge, close by these trees, we can bring the critters with us and make it all the way around to that barn on the far side."

I looked at the scene and shook my head. "No, too risky, too open, too close to the house." I looked some more and smiled.

"Well, sounds like someone's whistling a new tune. I take it you have a better plan, mister fancy book reader?"

"As a matter of fact, I think I do. Different, maybe. Better? Time will tell." I pointed. "There's the river below us. I figure if we angle southward a quarter mile or so, cut across the river, then head north on the opposite side, we can stay well away from the house. Then we can make our way to the barn and do as you said, hide Mossy and the bay there."

He said nothing, but eyed the scene.

I kept on. "With luck we wouldn't have to cross the river. But then again that fancy pasture fencing runs right down to that east bank in at least eight places. We'd spend most of the night dismantling it, and risk potshots from the house."

I shut my mouth then and let Jack chew on the notion. I knew it was the only way. Coming up behind the house was more direct, but too close and far too risky.

"Well." Jack scuffed gravel with his moccasin. "I reckon that'll work, too. Take us more time, though. I only suggested the other way because it'd get us into the thick of it a mite faster. Figured you want to get in there as soon as possible."

"I know it, and I appreciate it, Jack." I turned to scan the river, and hid a smile. It doesn't pay to let your friends know when you're grinning at their expense.

There was still about an hour before full dark. We could have started then, but that hour is a tricky one. Much of it depended on where the sun's rays struck. We would be well-hidden against the western shore of the river, but the trees weren't as thick there as on the eastern slope that led down to the river. That was the side where the ranch buildings sat. It was possible we'd cast long shadows. Any ripple in the light at all might catch the attention of someone looking from the house.

Hell, we didn't even know if it was them in the house, though my gut told me this was the place, and that was enough to go on for now. Like Jack said, if it wasn't them, we'd plead our case as weary travelers—not a big stretch—and move on.

We didn't know if it was just the two of them, the man and the woman, likely a couple, perhaps even married. Maybe they had henchmen waiting for them at the ranch. And where were they keeping Thomas? It was possible we'd passed him long ago, tied up and left to die, or already done away with. A single stroke or rock to the head, a knife to the chest, suffocation.

All these thoughts, coupled with the fact that I could think of no reason for them to keep him alive, made me one fidgety, sore-shouldered, woozy-headed, crack-ribbed fellow.

"Will you set down and finish your grub? Might be the last meal you ever have if half of what you're spouting is true." Jack snarled at me around a mouthful of food. "If we was to follow your dark trail of thought, we'll end up in the middle of a circle of gunmen a-bangin' away at us with all manner of weaponry."

He set down his plate. "I, for one, choose to think we'll muddle through it all somehow and come out smiling on the other end. Just now, I'm going to catch me a quick twenty minutes of downtime. My pins could use the rest, and so could my overused brain." He tugged a kerchief over his face. "It's the curse of a learned man such as myself, there ain't hardly no rest for yer thinker." In seconds he was snoring lightly, the faded red bandana fluttering with each breath.

I couldn't help but smile. For all I'd unintentionally put him through, I was mighty glad he was along for the journey. It occurred to me he never once said he'd do otherwise. Oh, he complained about everything and then some, but never about pitching in and helping me. And with no look for gain on his part. That's the mark of a true friend. I only hoped I could one day be as good to him.

CHAPTER EIGHTEEN

"Got to say, boy, all that mineral-rights palaver we got up to . . ."

"Huh?" I was paying more attention to the terrain than to Jack's chatter.

"You know . . . about these desperadoes being after the property for gold or some such useless gewgaw."

"What about it?"

"We might have been . . . oh, what's the word?"

"Premature?"

"Yeah, that."

Our whispered conversation continued sporadically like that as we picked our way toward the river. Then it took us nearly two hours to make our way across the river and northward along the far side of the bank. The icy water lapped chest-high on the animals and soaked me and Jack above our knees.

"Did I mention our cause was noble?" That was my weak attempt to smile at the dismal situation we found ourselves in.

"Noble cause or no," said Jack, spitting a mouthful of river water. It splashed into his face as the bay dug hard on the far bank to climb out. "We are long weary, wet as fish, sore as men can be and still be stumbling along, cold as blizzard babies, mind-numbed and bone-tired, and a hundred other ailments."

I thought he was done griping and was about to make another limp joke, when he sputtered and continued his hoarse-whispered tirade.

"And it ain't going to take much prodding for me to shoot someone, especially if that someone recently done me wrong."

I nodded in agreement, as I felt the same way. We spent the rest of the journey northward along the river in silence. It didn't much help that we knew we'd have to cross the river again to get back on the east side, where the ranch buildings sat all-but-invisible in the dark. Dim lamplight glowed in one window of the house. Somebody was still awake, doing something. It was too late and too dark for most folks to get up to much more than read or doze by a fire.

The air was cold and still, save for sudden gusts from the northeast. When the wind whipped across the pastures, crossed the river, and hit us it felt like the slap of a scorned woman, and it left us shivering.

I was hoping, with luck, we'd be able to make it all the way to the barn, spend the night in there, cold but out of the wind. Maybe warm up close to the animals, then get the drop on whoever might wander out of the house at cock's crow in the morning to tend the animals. It wasn't much of a plan, but then neither Jack nor I are much for planning.

We tend to bluster on in and deal with the situation as it arises. I don't think I picked up that trait from him. I have always been that way, but knowing he is of the same ilk has justified my own seat-of-the-trousers approach with much in life. I will admit it has not always proven to be the most fruitful nor wisest approach. But then again I am still alive, so it has worked so far. Never mind the various scars I sport on my homely hide.

"Remind me to throw you a beating when this is all said and done," Jack whispered.

We were close to the river again. Once we crossed, we'd have to cut the chatter.

"Oh," I said, "and here I was about to give you good news."

"What's that, river man? You going to tell me an ice floe's coming along to really seize up my joints?"

"No, but it looks like we won't have to get wet at all. Look." I nodded in the dark toward a wide, grassy hump stretched across the river. Wide enough for us to walk on, single file. They'd built a dam with what looked in the shadows to be an irrigation setup in the midst of it. This ranch was more impressive with each new discovery. Someone with a whole lot of money had dumped it all right here.

It was a pretty valley, to be sure, and it had to be close to an over-mountain road from the west. I was certain whoever built it didn't haul in their goods along the knobby, thin trail we took. It was also as obvious to me and to Jack that the place wasn't the mineral-rich wonderland Thomas was likely yearning for.

But it was a mighty promising ranch in a mighty pretty spot. A man could almost settle down in such a spot. Almost.

We made a whole lot more noise making our way up to the barn than I would have liked. But that's always the way when you're trying to be as quiet as a mouse in a house filled with cats. It didn't help that we ran out of soft grass and earth to walk on.

Somewhere along our path to the barn we did our best to stomp on every nugget of grating gravel as possible. Between the two of us and our two mounts, that was twelve feet menacing the still night.

The shadowed bulk of the barn, a broad, two-story affair with a handful of doors on the river side that opened into a paddock, blocked our view of the log house. The one dim glow from a lantern inside worried me. Who was still awake? Were they torturing him at that moment?

We succeeded in getting tight to the barn, though the house was the obvious spot for them to hold Thomas. Whether he was alive or dead was still a mystery—one I itched to solve. But it would have to wait until dawn drew closer.

"Reckon we can get in the barn?" Jack's whisper was low, but even at that it sounded like a shout in an echo-filled canyon.

I said nothing, but handed him Mossback's reins. That was my way of letting him know he was to wait there, in the trees to the north of the barn. Before he could shout a volley of whispers at me I crept forward.

Chapter Nineteen

Well, creeping might be what thin, small people do when they want to avoid detection. I have never been small nor thin. Then there was my wounded wing, still held in a sling, though I could use my hand pretty well. Toss in my ailing head that, though it was healing, I hoped, from the inside out, continued to be prone to quick bouts of unexpected dizziness. Mix all that up and you have a man who was doing his best to remain upright and not walk into great stacks of tin cans or step on a barn cat's tail. Neither happened on my way to the near side of the barn, thankfully.

I pressed one ear to the planking, heard nothing within, and groped the wall with a flat hand. The wood smelled good, dry and husky, like a fall campfire blended with the aroma of a fine pipe tobacco and maybe a cup of hot, spiced tea. I wondered briefly as I felt for a door handle what the inside of a tree smelled like to a tree. That led to comparisons with humans, and that bore quick abandonment. Funny what odd tangents the mind will follow, and at the oddest moments, too.

It was no time to wax philosophical. Fortunately I was saved from further flights of foolish thought by the familiar shape of a wooden slide latch. It felt about like all the others I'd encountered. A nub of worn wood no bigger around than a small finger jutted outward. I grasped it and slid to the right the small wooden bar it was attached to. Then I moved to the side, sliding my revolver from the holster, then nudged the door inward. It swung, the wood popping and squeaking softly.

No sunset-colored shotgun blasts bloomed in the night, no voices hissed a "Who's there?" at me. But I did hear a familiar low whicker. Tiny Boy. There would be other horses in there as well. Whatever beasts the man and woman had, plus Tiny Boy and Thomas's horse, and maybe the girl's horse, too. That made at least five.

In my experience, unless they're high-strung, horses are generally wary, but somewhat quiet if disturbed in the night. At least for a time. They're more apt to make a determination with their noses first. Sort of sniff the situation, as Jack might say.

I must not have smelled too threatening. Maybe Tiny Boy recognized me and somehow told the rest I was harmless. I don't know and at that point I didn't much care. I only wanted to get through the night, warm up as much as we could, and find out about Thomas.

I walked forward, my hand outstretched, and I stepped on something hard and flat. I bent down and my fingertips knew it for what it was—a book. It lay spine up, spread wide, mashed into the chaff-and-dung-covered floor. I suspected it was mine, but even if not, it should not be treated that way. Books mean too much to me. Of all the shifting earth under my feet at any given time, my fondness for books will not change.

If it was one of mine, I wondered, retrieving it in the dark and closing it gently, which might it be? *The Odyssey?* My new James Fenimore Cooper novel? That Dickens work I had reread numerous times? The *Holy Bible?*

I crossed the barn slowly, hoping it would resemble other stables with a main alley down the length of the middle and stalls to either side. So far, so good, I stepped again and again, felt something else hard and flat under my boot. Bent to it and yes, another book. Had to be mine. What had they done? Rummage through my belongings and toss away whatever they didn't want? My blood rose, but I kept on and reached the far end. Judging from the way this wall felt, it was a big double door with a smaller door set in it. That's probably what I had passed through on coming in.

I reached for the smaller door and found it after a few seconds of fumbling, right where I hoped it would be. I opened it a crack, looked toward the house, and saw no dim glow from the lamp. That bothered me more than seeing the lamp lit so late not long before.

I closed the door and hugging the wall on the river side of the barn, I felt along the front of the stalls. Something shuffled in the first stall, breathed roughly through its nose. A horse, but not mine. The same with the second and third, then in the fourth. I patted the air and was rewarded with a quick touch of a big, soft nose.

"Tiny," I whispered. He whickered and withdrew. We'd been together long enough to know each other's foibles. His was annoyance at being inconvenienced. It occurred to me in time that though he might be pleased to see me again, he was apt to show it as dismay. And that usually meant a bite. I pulled my hand away in time. There was a rush of air and I heard a quick, sharp click as his teeth came together.

"You big lummox," I whispered. "I'm here to rescue you." I didn't mention Thomas, as I was sure the horse felt the same way toward the greenhorn as everyone else did.

It didn't take Jack long to get fidgety and poke his head through the door I'd entered. "Boy? You alive?"

"Yep," I whispered back. "Chatting with Tiny."

"Well get the conversation over with. Time for us to lay low for a spell. I'm stiffening in this chill night air."

We led the bay and the mule in through half of the big door and decided to leave them loaded up, should we have to make a quick escape. Soon enough they dozed upright, and we all but did the same, so tired were we. I fought the alluring thought of sleep, insisting I take the first watch, but Jack waited me out and I fell asleep faster than I care to say. I don't know how long I was out, but it was still dark when Jack nudged me.

I rose silently, my joints popping and cracking as I stood. Jack dropped to his backside and leaned against the leg of a saddle rack. Within seconds I heard his rattle of soft snores.

It was warm in the stable, at least warmer than it had been dunking half our bodies in the river and then seizing up in the random breezes whistling through our holey clothes. I pulled in deep draughts of air through my nose to help clear the cobwebs of sleep from my head.

It worked about as it always did, which is to say not well. Nothing ever does when you're bone tired. But I managed to keep from dozing as I paced quietly, keeping an eye on the door at the far side of the barn that faced the house.

For their part, the animals were all quiet, dozing in the still air. I knew better than to pester Tiny Boy while he was still in a snit over what he no doubt was convinced was my abandonment of him.

As the barest light from sunrise slowly leaked into the barn, the shapes of walls, stall doors, a mound of old hay, a leaning shovel, and one broken-tined fork all became more distinct. I found another book—that made three. And they were all mine. Holding them close to my face I made out the titles: *The Odyssey*, the *Bible*, *The Last of the Mohicans*.

The spines had been snapped and the pages sagged, but they were in remarkably good condition for the treatment they'd received. I stuffed them inside the saddlebag on the horse. Then I toed Jack's foot and watched him wake as he always did—one eyelid popped open, the eye swiveling, confirming his situation before committing to full wakefulness.

He sat up, yawned, and stretched. "I don't think we ought to wait for someone to come on down here. These critters don't look all that well tended. Might be wiser for us to use early dawn to get to the house."

"Jack. I think I ought to go on up there alone while it's still dark, scout the place. I don't know what sort of condition he's going to be in. And besides—"

Jack interrupted with a horned hand. "I know, I know. He's your kin." He sighed, scratched his chin through his beard. "Be careful. We know what these folks get up to—they're evil and no mistakin' it. Now, check that revolver and get going while it's still mostly dark. I'll have the critters ready and I'll be covering you anyway with the rifle. It ain't that far and I'm still a fair hand with a long gun."

Even under cover of early morning, my creeping walk to the cabin was one of the longest I've ever taken. Each step uphill across the bare brown meadow—I avoided the graveled lane for fear of too much underfoot crunching—made me think of a story an old Irishman told me years before. I forget the nuances of the tale, but the gist was that only fools and heroes walk into their enemy's castle. I wasn't convinced I was the latter. On I blundered.

I saw no sign of movement, no slight shadows cross behind the windows, though it was still so early the sun had not yet crested the east ridge. My breath plumed from my mouth and I worked to keep it steady.

With each step I became more assured that the moment was pinching off, that any luck that had ridden on my shoulder had reached the end of its rope. Any second a fusillade would pummel me, leave my big body jerking and snapping in the yard before flopping, blood leaking into the brittle fall grass from a hundred puckered wounds.

At least that was the grim notion that refused to unseat itself from my mind. In truth, I reached the house, climbed the six steps, each one with an audible will of its own, creaking and popping, and me matching them with winces and gritted teeth.

It felt as if a lifetime passed before I finally reached the top of the steps, and leaned heavily against the log wall and its relative safety.

If they had locked the door from the inside, I was sunk, and would have to resort to peering in windows. Maybe I should bluster in, full-force, with the revolver barking for me.

But no, the door was unlocked. Why wouldn't it be? As far as they knew we were dead, so who else might pursue them? Perhaps they were waiting for the horse-faced man to return. They would have a damn long wait for that bastard to show his homely head again.

I slid the wooden latch, similar in construction to those on the barn, and with a fingertip pushed. The door swung inward and set up a grating squawk, long and loud enough to rouse a battlefield layered with dead men. Why don't people oil their cursed hinges?

I waited a long while before peering in, and then I did it at a lower head height than anyone waiting inside might expect a head to appear. It would buy me an extra second should it come to a fight. Always do the unexpected, especially in times of tension. It's a lesson I've learned the hard way over the years. I believe it has saved me a time or four. Or I have more of that feckless luck than any one man deserves.

When I finally peered into the dark room, I saw it as the kitchen and dining area, a big room running from the front to the back of the house. A large, fancy cookstove with nickel adornments hugged the wall separating the kitchen from the rest of the house. Beside it, a door stood nearly closed. To the left, a long dining table sat heaped with jumbled gear—cans, boxes, satchels, a sack of spilled flour. Some of the goods I recognized as mine or Jack's. If there had been any doubt before—of which there wasn't much—for certain we'd found our quarry.

Chapter Twenty

Dotting the table were several whiskey bottles, empties wedged every which way, a few on their sides, more on the floor. Beside those on the table stood several more, full and lined up as if awaiting orders, one half sampled. This might explain the sudden bucksaw snore from the far room. Whoever made it was likely hammering the depths of a deep drunk. I didn't envy them the full morning light fast approaching.

As my eyes roved the large, dim room, I saw Thomas a good dozen feet away, at the far end of the table. He sat strapped to a tall-back chair, his head flopped against one shoulder, bent so far it appeared as if his neck had snapped. I almost could have believed that dire notion had it not been for the steady in-and-out motion of his chest. He was breathing, probably asleep. Good. Any seconds I could gain not telling him to shush would be in my favor.

I paused, heard nothing at all save for the grating sound of a raven passing by the ranch on its way somewhere safer, no doubt. Then another ripping snore, then another, deeper in pitch, on its heels. Two folks then, dueling with snores. Had to be the man and woman. I could get the drop on them right then. Grinding my teeth together like I always do before I do something I know might be the last task I ever do, I inched my way into the gap of the open door.

It wasn't wide enough for me, naturally. I gripped the door tight and pushed, hoping the pressure would shut those hinges up for a moment. No luck. I paused once more, listening, watching. The snores had stopped. I waited, no sound, not even a ticking clock. Then I heard a snore, and its warring counterpart chasing it. I stepped into the room, decided to hell with any sounds from the floorboards. I would rush the far room, catch them in their sleep.

I wished they sped up their snores, maybe I could time my steps to help mask my footfalls on what I guessed, based on the thin early light streaking in, was a pretty orange-pine floor. I tried to take in each dark corner of the room as I walked.

I'd made it halfway across the room when a shout to my left, in the near-dark, froze me. I spun and saw Thomas head upright and struggling, shrieking as if he were being fried alive. Damn that kid. I lunged for him, reached out, and muckled onto his face with one hand. I managed to shut him up, though he struggled and snotted on my fingers.

"Shut up! Thomas, it's me, Roamer, now shut up!" I growled into his ear and it worked, he stopped thrashing. But as soon as he shouted, the dueling snorers in the other room came to life, thumping and shouting and crashing into Lord knows what.

The bedroom door whipped open, revealing a skinny man with gray hair tufting in all directions and bristly whiskers that had needed a trim a week before. He stared, arms wide, held out at the waist as if he were about to draw unseen six-guns. All he wore was a sweat-stained set of longhandles, pink-white in the early light.

"Hey! Hey!"

That seemed all he could say. Then as quick as he got out the words, a thick arm wrapped around him from behind and shoved him out of the way to pile up on the floor inside the dining area. The arm belonged to the woman, a plug shaped like an oak barrel, though she had sprung her stays in various places.

She wore little, her nightgown sheer from age, an unfortunate choice given that she was all rolls of fat and sloppy breasts. Atop them glared that face, the cruel visage I'd seen wearing Jack's lynx hat and mocking me, sneering down as Horse Face had shot me.

All this happened in the time it takes to draw a breath and let it out again. I'd begun to level the revolver on her, but from the shadows to her side she whipped up a double-barrel shredder. I dove backward, dragging Thomas down to the floor with me as the shot churned wood in the wall behind me. I heard shattering sounds, saw shards of plates fly through the air, and guessed it was a hutch of some sort that stood behind me.

I dragged Thomas further into the dark corner. He was screaming again, rocking back and forth, thrashing and fighting my efforts. I wanted to clunk him on the bean with the butt of the revolver, but there was no time for such indulgences.

Though the room rang—at least my ears did—with the explosive boom of the shotgun, I heard her thumb back the second barrel's hammer. That distinctive meaty clicking is no fun to hear if the snout of that gun is aimed in your direction.

There was a pause. I snatched up an empty whiskey bottle and tossed it toward the door. The scowling woman bit at the ruse and swiveled, touching off that trigger. Boom! Stink and sound warred for supremacy in the clouded room.

I didn't wait for her to reload. I was about to stand and send a few shots her way when I noticed the man wasn't there any longer. I figured he crawled back into the other room. The woman disappeared, too, but I heard her shouting and upending various items, no doubt looking for more shells.

Then thrashing and screaming, Thomas flopped into me. "I've been shot! Shot! Oh, God!"

All I wanted to do was barge into that room and put to rest those two bizarre creatures, especially that hateful sow of a woman. But if Thomas was truly injured, I had to get him out of there while I could. I also knew Jack was probably running across the yard, war cannon in hand, howling oaths that were turning the little valley's morning air bluer than the smoky room I stood in.

With a growl, I snatched Thomas, managed a chest full of shirt, and remembered he was tied tight to that chair. I didn't have time to cut him free—Jack had given me the girl's knife to strap on for my little adventure here—and I darn sure didn't want to waste the seconds I'd been given while the woman found more shells.

I dragged Thomas, in the chair, backward out the door, the revolver held poorly in my weak arm. When they opened up on me again, I'd have to figure out a different way of working. And I wouldn't have long to wait. I'd gotten Thomas out the door on the landing when she reappeared, shouting and sneering though the swirl of blue smoke. She raised the gun on me and I shoved Thomas down the steps, hoping he had sense enough to keep his head down below the tall spindles of the chair.

The shotgun blast blew the swung door half apart, exploding wood and driving splinters into my arms, legs, gut, and the back of my head. Thankfully I'd turned as I jumped for the ground. I wanted to drag Thomas out of the way and level off on her.

I crashed in a heap on the ground beside the greenhorn, who luckily hadn't broken his neck when I tossed him down the stairs. He lay there moaning and wagging his knees back and forth. As for me, I landed poorly, and on my gimpy shoulder. Hot pain bloomed fast and sharp, but there was no time to give over to it. The woman was emerging onto the landing, kicking at the blasted wreck of a door and cursing bad enough to make Maple Jack blush. Almost.

I realized then I'd lost my revolver when I landed. It couldn't be far, but I had no time to search. I flailed my good arm for the chair and shoved it and Thomas over, rolling on top of him like a shell on a turtle. I knew that was it, the next blast would peel my body apart. But maybe my bulk would finally be good for something, maybe it would save Thomas.

The blast came, a thunderous report, but not from the woman's shotgun. It came from nearby, from the direction of the barn and moving closer, and followed by a volley of shouts and curses. Maple Jack, cursing out a woman as he'd never done, I'm sure of it.

"Get up off your backside, boy, ain't no time for lallygagging. That she-devil won't stay cowed for long!"

He gimped on over in that peculiar rambling, swing-legged gait of his and stood by, his big revolver trained on the door above. I got to my feet, kicked something as I stood. It was the revolver. I grabbed it up, and muckling onto the back of the top cross-piece of the chair, I hoisted the still-whining Thomas aloft, onto my back.

"I got ya, now git!" shouted Jack.

Luckily Thomas is a slender fellow and the chair a spindly piece of furniture. I believe the ropes they'd trussed him with went a long way to keeping it from falling apart as I stomped back toward the barn.

"Far side of the barn!" shouted Jack, running half backward beside me. Then he stopped, leveled off, and let loose with another shot. I heard it strike wood, and from his cackles of glee, I knew he'd sent the foul woman scrambling back into the cabin.

I didn't waste time running through the barn, but kept on, reaching the far side from above. There stood Tiny Boy and Ol' Mossback, both saddled, and two more beasts behind them, the horse Thomas had bought for the girl to ride, and the bay Jack had been riding. The bay was loaded with what scant gear of ours we'd found in the barn. I silently approved Jack's choices.

I let the chair slide from my back to the ground, and caught it before it toppled to its side. I held it upright with one hand while I stuffed the revolver into the holster. I missed my own Schofield and gun belt. Had to be in the cabin. I'd fret over it later, but right then I had to contend with Thomas, who hadn't stopped howling since the crazy woman opened up on us in the cabin.

I sliced through the ropes binding his legs at the ankle to the lower rungs of the chair. Bad mistake, as the young fool began kicking out with those dandy boots of his, landing a couple of shots to my calf and shin.

"Stop it, you fool!" I bellowed right in his face. I imagine it was a whole lot like when I'd awakened to find a huge old silvertip boar grizz huffing and chuffing in my face. And I bet my breath wasn't any prettier than that bear's, either. I didn't care a whit, for it worked. The whelp kept his mouth shut, sobbing and hiccupping only when he couldn't control it.

Jack made it around the corner of the barn, smiling, and glancing behind. "They're holed up in there for the time being, tighter than a bull's backside. Ain't no way they're going anywhere. Besides"—he mounted up—"I turned the other critters loose. Be a while before they catch 'em, if at all!"

He was enjoying himself, and even though I felt like I'd botched the entire affair, I couldn't help but smile along with Jack. Of course, I had reopened my wound—blood had begun to sop through my shoulder bandage and show on my shirt— and got Thomas shot, or so he said (it sure didn't affect his kicking abilities).

We already knew the route we were going to take, straight northward paralleling the river, still to our left. There was a rough-carved road there, and since it was the only one we'd seen on this trip, we guessed it led eventually to civilization.

We had hoped we'd have the rank couple as prisoners or

draped over saddles, but given that Jack had mounted up and Thomas had settled himself in his own saddle, though still whining, I took it we were going to get on out of there for the time being, regroup our notions, and figure out what to do next. We were too frazzled to push the situation any more at that point.

At least Thomas was alive, I felt deep and tremendous relief at that. Despite the fact that he was annoying. We headed on up the road, confident we were not being followed. At least not by those two rascals. We'd gone a quarter mile or so when I said, "Whoa, whoa, hold up, Jack. I have to check on Thomas."

"What's the matter with him?"

"Said he was shot." Even my tone expressed my doubt. I shrugged and rode the few paces over to Thomas's horse.

"Where were you hit, Thomas?" I tried to sound concerned, though I don't think it came across that way.

"Here, look!" He almost shouted it as he held up his right arm and pointed at a fleck of red on his upper sleeve.

I leaned forward, squinted, leaned closer. "My word, you have been shot. If we don't get you professional medical help, you might not make it."

He looked up at me then, his eyes tearing. Maybe he was hurt more than he appeared.

"Scorfano, where is Carla? You remember . . . the girl?" He looked down at the saddle horn, at nothing. "Where is she? How is she?"

When I did not answer right away, he looked at me again.

"Later, Thomas," I said. "We'll talk about it later. We have to make time now."

We ranged another two, maybe three miles northward along the roadway, which by then bore sign of recent travel. It followed the flank of whatever arm of the Bitterroots these were, ranging up and away to our right, roughly eastward.

After my gentle ribbing and Jack's not-so-gentle chiding,

Thomas rode in sullen silence. I sent a few questions in his direction, but he was either so lost in his own mind he didn't hear me, or he chose to ignore me. I let it be. There would be time enough for questions—and answers. We needed lots of each. And the kid owed them to us.

It was a few minutes later when Jack stopped, nodded northward toward a raft of separating clouds. "See them peaks angling off eastward? You see that shaded gap there? No matter, I can see it. That's the pass, I reckon. It's still a good day or so from here, but that's it."

"The pass the Pend d'Oreille use?" I was intrigued. I'd only ever been along that way in high summer, and then only from the east. And not all the way through, either. But it was a pretty journey, good fishing, plenty of game. I wasn't so sure I wanted to do it in the winter, though. But if William Clark and Meriwether Lewis had traveled it, who was I to deny myself the experience?

"Yep. And that's a saw that cuts both ways. If it's as I suspect it is, and it is, then there will be a route west over Walla Walla way. Been on it a few times, trading and such. Hudson's Bay Company used to have a fine setup that way, on the Columbia River. Gone now, but they was good times."

"Jack."

"Yep, I recall one haul of furs—"

"Jack." I said it sharper this time, enough so that he stopped reminiscing and looked at me. So did Thomas. I nodded up the lane. Four riders headed toward us at a trot.

CHAPTER TWENTY-ONE

Jack and I spread apart a good dozen feet. We angled enough to cover each other, keeping Thomas behind.

"What do they want?" said Thomas.

"Your guess is as good as mine, boy," said Jack. "But I doubt it's an invite to tea." Jack drew his Dragoon, but kept it laid behind the saddle horn, cradled in his left hand.

They reined up close, about fifteen feet from us. Bold. The two outermost men, on the inside to my left, were working ranch hands. They wore sheepskin chore coats with large buttons, a few patches here and there, not uncommon, as ranch work had a way of snagging a man's attire.

Two were clean shaven, the third was working on a beard, past the point where it looked stubbled and lazy. They wore decent hats, and two of them had gloved hands. The newcomers' mounts were solid, a black, a roan, and two chestnuts, good saddle rigs, well tended.

I was used to taking in a man's general appearance at a glance, sizing them up should a situation evolve or, more to the point, devolve, into moments of required quickness.

It was their gun rigs that I was most interested in—all three men had unbuttoned those chore coats casually and revealed there were two lefties and a right-handed man. They held their hands knuckled down on their thighs in a way no casual man ever would. They all also carried rifles.

The fourth man, who looked to be the clan boss, was a wide-shouldered, stocky man. On foot he couldn't have stood more than five foot nine, wore a gray-and-green-plaid mackinaw with a turned-down sheepskin collar. His hands were gloved, and a fine, brown ranchman's hat, low crowned, sat atop a pepper-haired head. He kept himself trim, no hair on his face save for eyebrows and lashes and the beginnings of hairs curling out of his flexed nostrils like spider legs. Same for his ears.

There was nothing soft about the man. His eyes, a blue-gray, were clear, and took us all in at once. I could almost hear them clicking from one of us to another. His face was seamed from age, cracks trailed out around his eyes. His mouth was a lipless cut with frown creases angled down toward a block chin.

He looked to be about Jack's age, which is to say somewhere north of fifty, but how far I had no idea. He was a man used to work. He also wore no guns. But he did have a sizable coil of hemp rope thonged from his saddle horn, riding where a rifle scabbard would be.

Before I could beat Jack to a greeting—I have heard his greetings to flint-eyed strangers, and they are rarely words a fellow wants to hear—the brawny little boss man spoke up.

"I'm Scribley. You're on my land."

"It's a road, ain't it?" said Jack. I rolled my eyes, wishing his dander wasn't up.

"A road I built. I own the valley."

"You own the valley," echoed Thomas. I gave him a quick, hard stare but he had that blank look he'd worn since we spoke of the girl.

"Well, Mister Scribley," I said, forcing a smile and making certain my own hand was positioned near my revolver. "That's a convenient coincidence, as we are looking to ride through this valley. Now, if this is a toll road, that's a different matter. We'll gladly pay for the privilege."

"There will be no smooth talk."

He flicked his gaze from Jack to me as he spoke. He'd already guessed Thomas was no threat.

"You are trespassers at a time when the tally of horses on my ranch comes up short. Then we hear shots? That adds up to vermin in my midst. You are but horse-thieving trespassers to me."

"Now you hang on there, mister," I growled. "You have the wrong end of the stick."

He ignored me and continued talking in that hard, steel-on-stone voice. "And since I own this land, I am the law of this land. And as the law I mete justice as I see fit. You will be hung where you stand."

There was a moment of genuine silence, as if someone had blasphemed in the midst of a packed church. I know I heard the man correctly, but something in my mind howled with laughter. Had to be a joke. But no, those eyes and that mouth looked as though they'd never uttered a funny word and hadn't chosen this moment to begin.

"You son of a bitch!" That was Jack's preferred method of breaking the silence.

The rancher ignored him, reached for his coil of rope. "Who's first? I have work to do and I only have one rope. You'll take turns."

"Mister, if you think I'm going to get strung up by some two-bit strawboss rancher, you got a buildup of wax in your head. You better clean it right quick, 'cause I have strong words to say to you." Jack stood in his stirrups, his blotchy beard and hair framed a blazing red face and a mouth baring teeth a wolverine would be proud to own.

Something changed, the rancher's right eye twitched and his cheek muscles bunched as if he was chewing on something. "Boys," he said low. And faster than I would have guessed, those three ranch hands flanking the old chisel-headed dog shucked their weapons. Two palmed revolvers, while the one closest to me worked on whipping a carbine free of its scabbard so clean you would have thought he'd practiced it for a month for this moment. Maybe he had.

The only advantage I had was my distance from Thomas and Jack. Jack knew this and set up a quick diversion, heeling the mule into a fluster of stomping toward the side of the road. Two of the three armed men bore down on him. I wasn't worried about Jack or Thomas, who sat his horse, brows knitted as if he could not put a name to a face. I was only worried about the third man, he of the half-shucked rifle, who hadn't yet taken his eyes off me.

My revolver was only at half cock and though he shook his head slowly in warning, intimating that his rifle would do the speaking, he hadn't finished the process of slicking it out of the scabbard. He should have gone for his revolver.

I leaned wide to my right, thumbed that hammer back all the way, and drummed heels into Tiny Boy's ribs. He hates that and reacted with his usual vim—a burst of forward indignation. I used the moment to rake that whelp off his horse. He tried to shout but I caught him in the throat and it came out as a strangled gag. His rifle spun free of his grasp and clunked to the roadway dirt.

I didn't slow down, trusting that Jack would keep the festivities percolating. Oddly enough I heard no shots, but didn't have time to ponder it. I scooted Tiny Boy forward, jerked him in line right behind Scribley before the man deciphered a move.

When he did, it was to my advantage, for he angled his horse sideways between me and his "boys," the worst spot for him to have bumbled into.

I leveled the revolver steady on him, the snout but two feet from his hard head. There was not a drop of fear on his face. The only thing working were those jaw muscles and those hair-filled nostrils flexing in counterpoint with his slow, even breaths.

I chanced the quickest of glances at Jack and Thomas. Jack did as I hoped—he sacrificed his urge to fight for the chance I'd taken to get the drop on the boss. It worked, though I knew Jack, sitting on his horse with his hands up above his head, was one rankled old dog.

"You're a hard man, Mister Scribley," I said in a low growl, hoping my words would offend him. They didn't. He nodded and that jaw muscle bunched, let go, bunched again, as if he were chewing his terse words before expelling them. I waited.

The man I'd knocked to the ground had gotten a leg up and over his gasping. I heard the first breaths sucking back into his throat. I felt bad about it for a second or two. It's possible I hit him harder than I needed to. I tend to do that.

"I have earned it. Earned the right to be."

"I'm in no position to argue that. But to judge people before you hear them out? Based on, oh, let's see . . . no evidence? That's raw, mister. I don't believe I've ever stooped that low. Yet."

More jaw bunching. "You looking for a commendation?"

I chose to think that was his attempt at humor. I smiled. "No, not yet, anyway. But I am willing to turn you loose in exchange for a favor."

"Let me guess what that might be."

"You give us a listen."

"What about my men?"

"Tell them to back off. If you don't like what we have to say, we all agree to fill each other full of holes."

"Naw, boy," shouted Jack. "I'd rather take these two striplings on right here, right now!"

Nobody responded to Jack, which I am certain riled him further. If he were a rooster, all his feathers would be stuck out straight.

Rancher Scribley's jaw muscles worked double time. "All right, then."

It sounded like an admission of defeat. I had a feeling this man never backed down, never turned away until whatever he jousted with was dead or in agreement with him. I also thought he was honest, if a few degrees off true.

I nodded. "I'll turn you loose. You tell your men to do the same with my friends, then you get back on your end of the road, keep the guns holstered, and we'll palaver."

"Yeh." And he did.

As the tense moment loosened, I watched the eyes, the faces of his men. It was of interest to me that, to a man—even the one I'd worked over—I saw some measure of relief there, as if they had grown weary of Scribley's hardness and were glad of the reprieve. I don't believe I thought wishfully.

"Now," I said, once we were all assembled much the same as we had been before the silly fracas. "Where were we?"

The rancher wasted no time. He nodded toward me. "Speak your piece."

I was tempted to smile, but as I was certain to be the only one who found a vein of humor in this, I tamped it down and cleared my throat, but Thomas stomped all over my words.

"It's all my fault. I caused the whole cursed mess."

Jack and I looked at him in surprise. Thomas hadn't uttered six words since we rescued him and now he spoke fast, his voice trembling. With eyes tearful and wide, he looked at no one in particular, but at all of us, then the ground, the sky, the trees, back to us. He didn't make a whole lot of sense, but enough to get the story out. He drifted from mention of the deed to a ranch to his arrival in the town of Forsaken. At that, one of Scribley's men sneered.

"Forsaken's a hole." It was the one with the sore throat. His voice came out as a wheeze.

Anyone who's been to Forsaken would agree with him, but his boss cut him off with a glance. The man reddened and rubbed his throat, his other hand rested atop his saddle horn.

"What were you doing in Forsaken, boy?" said Scribley.

"On my way to my ranch. That's where I bumped into Scorfano."

"Who?"

Thomas pointed at me. His hand shook and his bottom lip followed suit. I felt as if I was at the receiving end of an accusation.

"We knew each other when we were younger."

Scribley nodded. That's when Jack, who had been twisting in his saddle and harrumphing and snorting like an old left-behind coon hound, reached his snapping point.

"Now, see here, this ain't getting us nowhere. Mister fancy-ranch-man, you and your boys ain't got no call to detain us! We're passing through."

"Jack," I said, hoping to prevent the coming trainwreck, but Scribley surprised us all and held up a hand.

"Man's right." He closed his eyes and pinched between his eyes. "I feel about as tired as you three fellas look, and that's saying something. If you were lynching material you would have made more sense by now. Come on up to the house and we'll see if we can't sort the chaff from the wheat over a bowl of hot stew."

And to prove his sincerity, Mr. Scribley turned his horse and waited for his three men to do the same. They all rode ahead of us on up the lane.

At best we'd reached the noon hour, and already the day had turned into one of the strangest I'd experienced in a long, long while. And it kept heading on the same course.

CHAPTER TWENTY-TWO

We were a tense and suspicious lot as we rode toward Scribley's place. Jack and I never swapped so many looks at each other's homely maws as we did on that few-mile ride. Were we riding into an ambush? Why the sudden turnabout on the rancher's part? And why weren't we getting the cold stare from his ranch hands as we rode?

Thomas had resumed his slumped-in-the-saddle pose, and didn't seem capable of stitching together words to form a sentence. I left him alone, but kept an eye on him. I was hesitant to dwell on what might have happened to him while he was in the hands of those two oddballs.

I also kept a sightline open behind us, difficult to do considering the road wound up and down, left and right through the upper edge of the valley. I saw no sign of anyone following. I was fairly convinced there would be no one back trailing us other than the two folks we'd confronted in the cabin. The woman, from what I'd seen, was the one who required watching. I guessed it was more the man who was a drunkard. Someone was—that table riddled with booze bottles didn't get that way by itself.

No matter, they didn't seem to have hired guns in their employ. So after a mile, while I didn't abandon backward glances, I concentrated my thinking, such as my ill-fed brain would allow, on the curious rascals ahead of us.

The landscape opened as we rode, not unexpected should

Scribley's boasts bear more teeth. Below and to our left coursed the river, and to our right, climbing gently upward to the rocky slopes of the Bitterroots, raw woods gave way to stubbled pasture. Each side of the road opened to well-groomed meadows speckled with the dried heads and rattly stalks of wildflowers and buff grass.

As we walked at a steady clip toward what we assumed was the ranch proper, those meadows tapered down to well-cropped pastures. Soon, those pastures were dotted with horses, finer horses I'd not seen all at one ranch. Buckskins, bays, Palouses, paints, and more, all well-fleshed and so handsome. Tiny Boy thought so, too. He chortled his approval, raising the heads of a number of stallions fenced away from the mares.

There were cattle as well, but horses were the main job here, that was plain to see. The cattle, though, were as well tended as the horses. Red and white in color—Herefords, I believe.

We worked our way past yet another curve and there sat Scribley's ranch house. The building itself was in construction not unlike the home at the previous ranch. But it was somehow cozier seeming, a point I found at odds with the demeanor of the man who lived there.

While we were still a short distance from the house Jack rode closer to me. I leaned over and listened.

"What say we cut bait and get the hell out of here? I don't trust that hothead any more than I do a hydrophoby polecat! Why, at any moment he's liable to whistle a new tune and unfurl his rope again."

I couldn't disagree with him, but I got the feeling the rancher was over his initial surliness. And I wanted to know more about the neighboring ranch. It seemed as if this man, with all the increasing evidence of his tidiness and efficient ways, had more than a passing connection to it.

"Aren't you curious about this Scribley fellow at all?" I asked Jack.

He looked at me as if I had one too many heads. "Nah. Seen his type before. He's a hard man in a hard country. Likely a few bad hands were dealt his way, now he's soured on the whole world. Blaming everyone for his troubles. All except maybe the person he needs to blame the most—himself."

"How'd you get so insightful, Jack?"

"Comes from not riding into fool situations." We rode in silence another few steps, eyeing the ranch buildings, and watching the backs of our former captors. I glanced at Thomas, found him the same, silent and dazed, as he had been minutes before. Maybe Jack was right, could be we were riding into a death trap.

Despite my hopes for a peaceable outcome, Jack and I kept our sidearms at the ready.

We rode by a large barn and the three helpers split off, angling toward a paddock beside it. They kept their backs to us and didn't appear threatening.

Now it was us and the rancher. What were his intentions? He rode right up to the hitch rail before the house and swung down stiffly. He still didn't look at, nor address us. We sat our mounts, Jack angling to take in the entire yard should the hands set upon us in ambush. None came.

Finally Scribley rested a hand on the near stirrup and looked up at us. "You have the right to be skittish around me, I understand that. But I won't be threatening any of you with the rope, nor with anything else, for that matter."

None of us moved.

He sighed. "I suspect it won't help much if I were to tell you that once I change my mind I do not change it back. Anyway, it's time for hot stew."

With that he walked up the four broad steps leading to his

wide front settin' porch and waited at the top. I made the first move and nudged Tiny Boy over to the rail. As a small kindness to the rancher, I tied him well away from the man's own horse. Tiny can be testy with new acquaintances.

I walked over and led Thomas's mount to the rail. Finally, Jack, who had also been leading the bay, dismounted and made his way over, one hand on the revolver wedged in his waist sash, one leading his mule. He looked as excited to be there as a dance-hall girl in a house of worship.

Speaking of buildings, the cabin was a sumptuous-looking affair, long and low, too shaded for my tastes by the wide porch, but with plenty of windows. A trait shared with the other place. The interior was warm, snug, and well appointed. The honeyed-wood of the interior was filled with comfortable chairs and all manner of richly carved sticks of furniture not made on the premises—unless the surly rancher happened to be an Old World craftsman.

As to Scribley, he went about stoking the stove and thumping a wooden spoon on the hot rim of a big cast-iron pot. The vessel soon began to give off the unmistakable warm smells of home cooking. And my ample gut gave off its own response by way of grizz-cub growlings. Jack's followed suit. Pretty soon it sounded as if our paunches were fighting it out in a cinched feed sack.

If Scribley heard, he made no mention. Though I fancy I saw one corner of his tight-set mouth twitch. The bud of a smile? Not impossible, I'd like to believe. He directed us to a soapstone sink with a hand pump, and set out a stack of clean hand towels. Then, again as soundlessly, he directed us over to his table. We all sat near one end, closest to the big cast-iron stove, and he dished out some of the tastiest venison stew I have ever had. By the way he tucked in with his customary vigor, I could tell Jack enjoyed it, too.

Before we commenced, I paused, thinking for certain that the rancher was going to bow in prayer. He did not and I found this curious. I had him pegged as a religious sort. But then again, he might well be, in his own way.

I consider myself spiritual, though not necessarily enamored of a particular church or persuasion. The out-of-doors is my church and the amazing sights and smells and sounds I experience as I travel are proof enough to me that something larger than me exists.

I tend to keep all this to myself because I have no desire to have religion foisted on me by others. I imagine a fair lot of other folks feel the same way. In fact, a thoughtful relationship with the deepest part of themselves is about as true as a man or a woman can get in life.

For some that takes the form of religion, for others, the quiet calm of a mountain meadow as the morning sun steams off a scrim of thick dew.

As I ate I glanced across the table at Thomas. The boy was troubling me. He had been acting strange for far too long. Had they hit him in the head and dizzied him up? That would certainly account for his odd, quiet demeanor. Though more than likely it was his suspicions of what had befallen the girl.

When we'd plowed through a bowl of stew in silence, the man ladled out a second helping for all, then sat down. He rested his forearms against the edge of the table and looked not at us but up past the hanging oil lamp toward the low squared beams of the ceiling.

"As I mentioned, my name is Scribley, Clement Scribley. I am a bachelor. I came to this valley nearly twenty years ago, though I was not alone." He spooned up a bit of stew, chewed, swallowed. It was plain he would continue, and he did.

"I paid a terrible cost to get here. I am the last of three brothers, the only Scribleys left after the foul war. We brothers were

determined to establish a ranch and prosper. To begin anew
with families of our own." The earlier firmness of his voice was
now tinged with a slight waver.

"It was our intention to find such a place as this, one that offered plentiful water and timber. We had grand designs of building up a vast ranch, running the range with a mix of horses and
cattle. And that has come to pass. There is good forage for them
here, as you have seen for yourselves."

His eyelids drooped again and the surly expression of earlier
clouded his face, his voice matching it. "One of my brothers
died along the trail out here of a fever. The second less than a
year after our arrival, in a skirmish with bandits."

He worked his jaw muscle hard then, as he stared at the
sunset glow of the oil lamp hanging above the middle of the
table. "After all that, I was determined to make a go of it here,
alone if need be. And for much of a year following, I was alone.
Then I was able to hire help, and little by little built up the
ranch while fending off all manner of hazards—Indians, rustlers,
common thieves."

He looked at me then. "You can see why I was wary of you
earlier. Especially with how you look and those gunshots we
heard."

"You got a nerve, mister, commenting on how we look." Jack
puffed up, but still managed to soldier on with his stew.

"Jack," I said, hoping to head off a tirade. "It is true, we are
not the prettiest pair of backwoodsmen a person is likely to
meet."

"Just what have you been through?" Scribley said.

A fair question, considering we looked chewed on, smelled
rank, and were partaking of the man's fare. "Well sir." I wiped
my mouth with my hand, nodded toward the front wall of the
house, the direction we'd come from. "It's a long story, as

Thomas nibbled at earlier. Has to do with that ranch back there."

Scribley sat up straighter, still staring at me. "I had a feeling you weren't riding through."

Jack snorted, but kept chewing.

CHAPTER TWENTY-THREE

Scribley stood. "Well, let me tell you what I know of that place, then, since you are about to ask anyway." He poked the wood in the stove, added two pieces, then plucked down four squat drinking glasses from an open shelf above the sink and set them on the table.

He turned to a cupboard and brought down a bottle of liquid the color of red hair in the sunlight. The label was in French, but I did pick out the word *cognac*. The rancher didn't even ask, but poured four glasses and nudged one to each of us. Then he sat and resumed talking. Time was something Mr. Scribley had figured out how to take slowly.

"It had been my intention from the start to stake claim all the way down the river, including the land that ranch sits on. And I did, too, though it was an undertaking that caused considerable pain to my coin purse at the time."

"When was this?" said Jack, who had warmed considerably when Scribley brought out the bottle. It was possible we'd even see Jack smile before the night was out.

"I'm getting to that." Scribley sipped, then spoke again. "In order to establish certain arms of my business, I needed capital. I had put myself in a position I did not want to be in. But as I say, it was one of my own devising, so to speak. Along about that time, a wealthy man, one Abraham Rawlins, from back East, Providence, Rhode Island, to be precise, ventured out here with a guide and fell in love with the valley. In particular that sloping river meadow that ranch now sits on.

"He offered to buy it, and a sizable chunk of land surrounding it, from me, for a substantial amount, a figure I could not turn down. More than I would need to continue with plans of broadening my empire, so to speak. I would be able to irrigate, grow crops, employ more workers, breed fine horses, and establish extensive logging operations. The world, I felt, was finally opening to me."

Hell, with all his downright chattiness I wondered if we'd see a smile from Scribley, too. I made a wager with myself to see who cracked first before the night was out, Maple Jack or Clement Scribley.

"In short, I sold it to him. Enough land so that he felt as though he had a special spot all to himself. And what's more, he wanted me to continue as steward of the property."

"Sounds like a good deal all around," I said.

Scribley nodded. "He was a curious sort of man, had always wanted to come out West, but for many years had been, as he put it, burdened with too many family members dependent on him. Ironically, his was the opposite situation as mine."

He sipped, fell silent for a few moments, then spoke again. "He was also making too much money to leave."

"Nice problem to have," said Jack, color riding high on his cheeks.

I looked to Thomas, but he was fingering the sides of his glass, lost in his thoughts.

"To be sure," said Scribley. "He made his fortune in ice, of all things. A commodity that melts. Amazing. His clients were primarily shipping companies with great fleets of schooners plying the coast and the oceans with perishable goods. He made it out here and hired me and my men. He also brought in a selection of craftsmen of his own to build the place. I'm not sure if you noticed, but he spent a fortune there. It's nice enough, but

I prefer my own home." He looked around the friendly room, his relaxed face matching the warmth of his abode.

Such a contrast to the man's earlier attitude, I thought.

Jack nodded. "I've rarely seen its equal. Especially out in the wilderness as it is."

"It is a curiosity. But he had money and the inclination."

Jack leaned forward over the tabletop and squinted. "What's with all this palaver we heard about mineral rights?"

Scribley eked out a small smile then—I owed myself a penny—and nodded. "That's a rumor the old man started. Thought it would make it sound more dashing and authentically Western in his letters back home. I remember him chuckling as he told me about what he wrote to family members back there. In truth, he was happy to live there, had a woman who cleaned and cooked for him, and her husband kept the stable. They were former slaves, as a matter of fact. Good people. They made a cozy little setup for themselves inside the stable. All in all, I believe Mister Rawlins had a fine time there. Just not a long one."

"What happened to him?" said Jack.

"Early one April morning, we still had plenty of thick snow covering everything, the stable man, Jordan was his name, rode up hell for leather, shouting for help. Well, a pile of us rode back down there, for we were all fond of Rawlins, but there was nothing for it. He'd died with a cup of coffee in his hand, setting in his rocking chair on that porch. He was waiting for his breakfast and looking out as the light came up over the valley. And believe it or not, there was a smile on his face."

"Good a way as any to go." Jack grunted.

Scribley nodded. "And a damn sight better than most others." He pulled in a deep breath, let it out slowly, and resumed his story. I noticed Thomas was now watching him, too.

"It wasn't long before Jordan and Beulah moved on. Mister

Rawlins had left them a tidy bit of savings. As they passed on through this way they told me they were headed for the coast, then would make their way northward to Canada. I wished them luck and have not heard from them since. That was nine years ago."

"And the ranch has sat empty this entire time?" said Thomas, who had not uttered a peep since the road.

Scribley looked at Thomas, then nodded. "Until now."

Thomas's eyes focused and he glared at our host. I thought he was angry, but he held up a finger, said, "Scribley!" and reached into his coat.

CHAPTER TWENTY-FOUR

The rancher, and I could hardly blame him, flinched and he squawked backward in his chair, as if to prepare himself for an attack.

But Thomas only rummaged his hand around in the ragged folds of his garment, pulled it out empty, his shoulders dropping along with his brief near-smile. He folded his hands before him on the table.

"Thomas," I said, quietly. "What were you doing?" I suspected Jack and the rancher regarded him, as did I, as someone whose boat had become untethered and was now adrift.

He shrugged. "The deed." He looked up at Scribley. "You are mentioned in the deed, sir."

"What? What deed? What are you talking about?" The rancher looked at once perkier and more suspicious than I'd seen him all day.

Thomas sighed and closed his eyes. "Since we are sharing long-winded stories, and since it feels as if you are owed an explanation, at the least for your hospitality, if not for your demeanor, I will endeavor to explain to you how I came to possess the deed to the ranch at which I was so recently held captive."

I was not certain how to take this sudden flurry of words from Thomas. On one hand I was pleased to hear he sounded as if he had regained control of his faculties. On the other hand, he was back to his old less-than-tactful, pampered-rich-child self.

"My father was an important personage." Thomas's eyebrows rose and he cocked his head slightly in Scribley's direction.

The rancher nodded his head slowly, unsure of what to make of the sudden appearance of this odd person in his midst.

"He was a nobleman in Italy," resumed Thomas. "And to make a long and rather exciting story short for the sake of brevity, if not levity." He smiled at his own wit. No one else did. Thomas did not notice. "At the behest of the president of the United States himself, my father emigrated to America to orchestrate maneuvers, plans, and strategies for various covert causes. Already a highly decorated warrior across Europe, he was also a recognized and brilliant tactician."

"What does any of this fooferaw have to do with the ranch, boy?" This time it was Jack who had lost all patience with Thomas's windy ways. I nodded my support.

"Oh fine, then, if that's the way you want it. My father ended up coming into possession of the deed in question, and so passed it to me as my inheritance shortly before . . . before he, ah, was once again called away on important and highly confidential military orders, this time away from the shores of America."

I watched him, wondering if he was about to divulge that the old man, that is to say our father, had died. I did not care to see Thomas, maudlin and weepy, at this stranger's table. "To the point, Thomas," I said.

"Yes, yes, as I was saying." He directed a fiery look my way. "I decided that in order to lay claim to my inheritance I should see it myself, in person, and make a grand adventure of it. And that is what I have done, eh, Scorfano?"

I couldn't take it anymore and stood, knuckling the table and staring across at him. "If that's what you call getting people killed, two others robbed and nearly killed, homes burned, getting yourself kidnapped, getting us shot at, then threatened with a lynching, well then by all means, refer to this dandy little trip of yours as a grand adventure."

My heavy-handed reaction had more to do with the fact that the little ungrateful cur was my brother than because his story was boring. I shouldn't have, but I felt guilty about everything that went south on the whole ill-bred venture.

There was silence for a few moments, then Mr. Scribley cleared his throat. "I can piece together the rest. Now, young man, you say I am mentioned in the deed. In what way?"

"The right of first refusal."

Scribley half rose. "You mean it's in there? In writing?"

Thomas nodded. "I cannot tell a lie. But as I no longer have the deed, it is of little consequence."

"But that copy of the deed is not all that relevant, a mere formality," said Scribley. "It is recorded elsewhere, surely. I had no idea Mister Rawlins had actually put that in his will, his deed. I had, of course, asked him to please extend me that courtesy, but then he died and I believed all hope of purchasing that property was gone. I tried, naturally, but received no response."

"Well, as I said, sir." Thomas steepled his fingers, trying to look as if he were in deep concentration. "Those . . . reprobates who kidnapped me, hurt them." Here he nodded at Jack, then me. Then his face went white and I thought he was going to weep, but he regained his composure. "It's the papers, you see. They have it all now."

"I doubt that," I said. "As Mister Scribley mentioned, they may have a copy of the deed, but that is all. Apparently you are the legal heir to the property."

"That's the problem." Thomas dropped his head into his

trembling hands, raked his curly brown hair in fear and frustration.

"Boy, what are you talking about?" It was Scribley that time, annoyed with the emotional, nonsensical turn this conversation had taken.

"The papers, they state explicitly that the bearer of the original document is the sole owner. I didn't give it much consideration until I got out here in this . . . this vast ocean of viciousness and carnage and . . ."

"All right then, enough of badmouthing our home, Thomas," I said, for I consider all of the West my stomping grounds. "I still don't think there's much to worry about, though I can't fathom why they kept you alive, considering they're so murderous where the deed's concerned."

Jack piped in. "Maybe they're not sure of themselves, intended to keep the boy alive until they knew for certain he wasn't vital to their schemes."

That made some sense, as much as any of this deal made, anyway. "Maybe so," I said. "But where that deed's concerned, I can't imagine such a clause would hold up in a court of law. After all, there is certain to be a copy of it back East."

Thomas shrugged. Not an encouraging sign. "I've never heard of the existence of one. But that really doesn't matter now. We have bigger problems."

Jack sighed and ground stubby fingers into his eyes. "Boy, you know something more about all this foolishness, you best come out with it. You are testing my patience."

"And mine," I said.

"Count me in." Scribley downed the last of his drink and clunked the glass on the wooden tabletop.

"Fine, then." Thomas cleared his throat. "That wasn't the only clause your Mister Rawlins put in the deed. Apparently in an effort to ensure whoever ended up with the ranch wouldn't up and sell, he also included a thirty-day occupancy clause wherein the possessor of the deed must stay on for a month."

"That old Mister Rawlins, he might have been a savvy businessman with his ice and all," said Jack. "But it sounds to me he was a whole lot shrewder about folks and their fickle ways." Jack cast a look at Thomas, but the intention was lost on him.

Scribley nodded. "I'll bet that clause was directed at his money-grubbing relatives back East. He told me more than once that if they wanted anything from him after he was dead, they were going to have to earn it. Then he'd wink."

"Got to respect a man like that," said Jack, sipping the last of his cognac. "Who knows? After a month there, it'd be the rare person who wouldn't want to stay on."

I looked at Thomas, but saw no sign of agreement or disagreement on his face. "Thomas, you need to tell us about your captors." I couldn't let the matter drop, scurry off to the mountains, and live my life run off by two such as them. Not when we had all lost so much, the girl the most of all. "Thomas, we need to learn more about them. There might be something you know that will help us deal with them, short of going in there with brute force and taking over."

"Brute force is exactly how I aim to deal with them," said Scribley.

"Where the deed is concerned, they have the law on their side," said Thomas.

"Aren't you forgetting they are lawbreakers, the worst kind?" I said it through gritted teeth as images of the dead girl clouded my mind—slowly swinging from the tree, her kicked-off boot, her blue face . . .

Scribley must have sensed my anger, and cleared his throat. "From what you tell me, with all the chicanery those two have gotten up to, I don't think the law will do much to go against us. And besides"—he stood, razed a hand along his chin—"I am the law in these parts."

"Don't think we've forgotten that, Scribley." In word it was a kind remark, but the way I said it intimated it would be a long time before I would forget what he'd threatened to do to us. Jack nodded agreement with me. If the remark mattered to Scribley, he didn't let on.

"Well," said Thomas, swallowing and looking around the table.

"Speak up, boy. Lamp oil isn't free you know." The rancher had slipped back to his bold, no-nonsense self.

"Yes sir," said Thomas. "There are two of them. Felix Meiderhoff and his wife, Esmerelda. He once called her Ezz in front of me. But only the once."

"The once?"

Thomas shrugged. "I'd say she didn't like it. She hit him and he didn't call her that again." He leaned forward over his glass. "She is a frightening woman."

I recalled what I'd seen of her, and while I wouldn't have referred to her as frightening, I can say she was coarse, and sloppy, all scowl lines and flinty eyes. And when she did smile it was a cruel look, uncomfortable on her low, homely face. She looked to be the sort of woman who is never happy in life.

"What about their drinking, Thomas? Which one is the drunkard? Or is it both?"

"They both imbibe," he said. "But Mister Meiderhoff is the one with the problem."

"Hitched to a cow-beast like that," said Jack, looking wistfully into his own empty glass. "I don't blame the man for taking to the bottle."

"Before I light out in the morning to settle their hash once and for all," said Scribley, "I'd like to know the details of how your father came by the deed, young man. Is that information you have?"

Thomas looked up at Scribley, who had advanced to the youth's chair and looked down at him, arms folded across his chest.

"I don't know the answer to that, sir. I have given it some thought, particularly since this adventure began to sour. My best conjecture is that he bought it from one of the old man's heirs, perhaps one who hoped to make quick cash."

"You ever consider he might have come about it unlawfully?"

"Papa?" Thomas pulled back as if struck in the face. "Never. You, sir, do not know my father. He was a man of high moral standing and of kind temperament to all he ever encountered."

I stifled a snort, turned away to hide the mask of incredulity that had crawled over my face.

Thomas continued droning on in his puffed-up way. "You will have to travel far before you will find someone who may have an unkind word to say about my papa. And even then, I would doubt their veracity."

Again, I struggled to suppress snorts of derision, turned them into coughs and gagging sounds—not far from how I felt.

"Get yourself a cup of water, Roamer. Get me one, too, whilst you're at it." Jack stretched back in his seat and yawned, a smile wide on his face. He was enjoying the proceedings.

"Legally speaking, I don't have much of a leg to stand on," said Scribley. "But I'll not have such people living next to me. Especially not when I should lawfully be allowed to buy it back. I have plans for that land, better plans than those rascals would have."

"You could wait them out," said Jack. "Give them a month, then make 'em an offer."

"No," said Scribley, shaking his head. "People like that are never satisfied with an offer. They will want more and more.

And the biggest fear I have is that somehow they might find someone who would meet their extortionist demands."

No one said anything, then Scribley splashed another round into all our glasses. "Besides," he said, sipping his. "I still have hopes of handing off this ranch to my own children one day."

"You married?" said Jack, looking around the house as if he expected to see a wife and children pop out of the dark corners and shout, "Ta-da!"

"No . . . no." Scribley looked a pinch red in the face. It was obvious he'd said something he regretted. Or it could have been nothing more than the stove he'd hotted up again, or the cognac. More than likely, though, it was the admittance he'd made to us, three strangers in his home.

"I am an older fellow, I recognize that and admit it. But I still have hopes of luring a young woman out here under entirely honest terms with an eye toward her becoming my bride. When I pass on I would like to know there will be other Scribleys tending the land, this place, long after I have gone. Yes, a good, hardworking woman from honest stock. Perhaps she won't have much of her own, but won't mind being saddled with an old man who can still"—he sipped his drink—"still, ah . . ."

"Garden at night," said Jack, straight-faced and nodding.

"Yes, yes, that is precisely what I mean."

There was silence once more while we all sipped and pretended what we'd heard was not awkward. Well, maybe not for the two older gents. They seemed in quiet agreement. As for me, Scribley's admittance went a long way toward helping me regard him in a more kindly fashion. It seemed he was human after all.

He interrupted the quiet, addressing Thomas once more. "Son, if you can get that deed back into your own hands, that shows you're the rightful owner, then, regarding my initial offer I made to my old friend, Abraham Rawlins, I'll honor it and extend it to you. On the other hand, should you want to take it over and ranch it yourself, why I . . . I won't blame you, of course. Though I hope you will consider my offer in all seriousness.

"I will make no effort to disguise my lust for that property, as should be well apparent to you by now, young man. I dream of owning it once more, have for nearly ten years. I've sent a flurry of letters all over the map in an effort to determine the land's status. Alas, no family members of Rawlins gave me the time of day. Now, that is neither here nor there. At least now I know more than I did yesterday and for these past years."

Thomas said nothing, but his eyes were clear, not skittery and unfocused as they had been. The opportunist in him had taken it all in.

CHAPTER TWENTY-FIVE

Jack slipped out the front door. I gave him a minute, then followed and found him standing on the porch overlooking the dark dooryard. A breeze worked its way through the tops of the ponderosas, then moved on.

"You know we don't owe this fella, don't you? We got what we came for, saved the boy."

I said nothing yet. I knew he wasn't done.

"When did you get to be a big softy, anyway? Since when are other people's problems your problems?"

By his tone Jack was still festering about the near miss with the lynching. I did not disagree. "You having second thoughts about what you said in there?"

"I ain't one to back away from much, especially a situation such as this. It reeks like a month-old grizz-kill carcass."

"But?"

He sighed. "It's been a long week, Roamer. I am frazzled. I been rode hard and denied my oats. Don't like to admit it, but there it is."

"I understand, Jack. I really do. But I can't leave Scribley with those murderous bastards so close. Besides, they still have our gear. And you saw what they did to my books. To me, that alone is worth running them aground." I clapped a hand on his shoulder. For such a solid fellow, he felt thinner, older. Odd how a rum run will do that to a person. "I respect your opinion no matter what you choose, Jack. Do what you need to."

Quick as a startled cat, Maple Jack whipped his mangy maw around and poked me in the chest with a steel rod of a finger, a sure sign I'd stepped in something I should have avoided.

"Respect my opinion? Oh, Lordy, you worry me, boy. You really got me concerned—I got to tag along on this harebrained plan to make sure you don't get yourself kilt! Any softer and you'll need a dress and fancy parasol. Respect, I ain't never heard the like."

I smiled in the dark, feeling no need to take offense to his tirade. I had given him the excuse he needed to back away from that comment about being frazzled. I knew he'd wished he'd not given voice to it, even if it was the truth.

If we made it through the next couple of days, I vowed to make certain Maple Jack had a chance to ease up, put his feet up, and maybe whoop up at a settlement or town somewhere along the trail.

Scribley sighed and shook his head when I told him we would be heading back to the ranch the next day. "Provided you let us bunk in the stable for the night. We're tuckered."

"Son, I don't know you or that youngster, Thomas, nor your friend, Maple Jack, but I can tell you I won't think ill should you want to move on. This is not your tussle. I'll get the boy's deed back and hand it over, rest assured. I shoot straight in all my dealings, ask my men."

"You're dead wrong, Mister Scribley. It's more our tussle than anyone else's." Before he could protest I pushed on. "Besides, it's not about the deed so much, Scribley. As Jack said earlier, those bastards have caused us each no amount of trouble. They shot me, left me for dead, and stole my gear. They burned Jack's cabin and stole his goods. And one of their confederates left a girl dead. We did for him, but it's been a hard business. So if you'll excuse me for saying so, this deal is more our business than it is yours."

I dragged a paw down my stubbled jaw and kept on. "And what's more, we'll be the ones riding ramrod on it. If you and your men care to throw in, I won't say no to the help. Only thing is . . ." I leaned in and lowered my voice, hoping Thomas wouldn't hear me. "I'd as soon Thomas not be mixed up in this. He's no gun hand and I don't want him hurt. Maybe he could wait us out here."

Before Scribley could reply, Thomas shoved back from the table. "See here, Scorfano. I heard that and I am quite capable of taking care of myself. There is no reason to whisper in the shadows about me as if I were a child to be toddled off to bed. No, sir, I will not tolerate it. I am part of this venture. Indeed, I am the reason we are here in the first place."

"Well, thank you, laddie, for owning up to it. 'Bout time, too," said Jack, coming in from out of doors.

The rancher said nothing, eyed us each in turn, then nodded his head and offered us comfortable accommodation for the night under his roof. Despite Scribley's protests and offers of ticking mattresses and spare rooms, Jack and I kindly refused, preferring to bunk in the stable. I've spent far too many nights camped with Tiny Boy to be comfortable in a house. And though Jack had a cabin—used to, anyway—he only slept indoors when freezing temperatures and deep drifts of snow made dozing by the campfire out front of his place an uncomfortable labor.

As for Thomas, he readily accepted Scribley's offer. This did not surprise me, and in truth I was relieved. It would keep the youth safe and away from me. I was still far too angry with him to spend the night listening to him whine about a sore backside.

"First light I'll have breakfast rattling. All my men come in of a morning and we start the day here at the big table. I find it to be an efficient way to tally the day's needs."

Not long after we'd set down to the evening's meal, Scribley told us he'd ordered his men to put our beasts up in the barn, rub them down, feed them. I had gone to check on the situation, to be certain, but all had appeared as Scribley said.

So now, with the help of a lantern supplied by the rancher, we made our way to the barn. It didn't take long to find our beasts. A thorough perusal convinced us they had been treated much the same as we had—rubbed down, fed oats and sweet-grass hay, and put up in fine stalls. Our gear was stacked neatly and unmolested, and our tack set on nearby racks.

We bedded down outside the stalls. Despite the creeping cold of night in high country, we were snug and warm in our blankets. We each laid a few spare saddle blankets on top of us, nested deep in ample piles of clean hay, and set to sawing logs right away.

CHAPTER TWENTY-SIX

I have no idea how he does it, but Maple Jack can be dead to the world tired and scrape up but an hour or two of deep slumber. Then he'll snap awake before dawn as if kicked in the seat, every single morning. On my own, I will rise when I hear morning sounds—birds fidgeting and chattering at each other in the trees, squirrels cursing everything under the sun, other rodents rummaging in the leaves. Often, Tiny Boy, hobbled close by, will make his way over and nudge me if he feels he's not been attended to in a timely manner.

"Boy. Hey, Roamer." It was Jack, toeing me with his moccasins. Times like those I was thankful he had a lifelong aversion to hard-sole boots.

"Get up, and I won't say it again. I see light through the windows at the house, and if that rich ranchin' bastard can cook up a breakfast spread as good as his stew, we're in luck." For emphasis he smacked his hands together and let his paunch growl away as if he'd trapped another starving bear cub in there.

We made our way back to the house, much refreshed after a decent sleep in a comfortable spot. We clumped up the steps following a couple of hands we hadn't met before. A few more came after us. Not a one seemed interested in us or surprised at our appearance around the breakfast spread.

And what a spread it was: stacks of big, steaming flapjacks, thick smoked bacon fried enough to draw out the flavor, a mess of golden eggs, plenty of hot coffee, thick and strong, and even a pot full of porridge. Plus sugar, butter, salt, and pepper. I wasn't about to complain.

Mr. Scribley had help at the stove and in a back room I took to be part of the kitchen. A young cowhand I'd seen eyeing us from off by the barns when we rode in the day before now wore a soiled white apron and a red, smiling face as he dished up good food.

I don't know when he did it, but it appeared that Scribley had already told his men about us, for they were a jovial bunch and included us in their conversation. Scribley nodded toward the young aproned man. "That's Jasper. He's learning his way around the kitchen. We all take turns at feeding time."

"Good way to be," said Jack, between bites of butter-dripping flapjack. "A man who can't cook ain't got no business eating in the first place," he said, to a chorus of nods and grunts of approval. Nobody said much as they were all busy eating. A feed like that every day would go a long way to convincing me I needed to bed down at that ranch for the winter.

Thomas, who had shown up late to the breakfast table, still in a nightshirt, likely loaned from Scribley, and looking as though he wanted more hours of sleep, took a seat at the end of one side of the long table. He nursed on a cup of coffee and seemed unaware of the men or the discussion going on around him. I thought not for the last time what a strange young fellow he was. Raised rich is how Jack had described the youth's malady. I agreed with that simple assessment.

The men at the table were too polite to comment on their boss's houseguest, though I did spy a couple of them suppressing smiles and shaking their heads. For his part, Thomas remained oblivious and aloof.

We weren't halfway through the meal when boots hammered up the steps. None of us had time enough to do much else than turn our heads, coffee cups in hand, when the door slammed inward.

"Riley, what is the meaning—"

But Scribley's rage was cut off by the newcomer. "Sir," the man breathed hard, red-faced, and yanked his hat off, torturing the brim as he stood in the open door. "Hard cases rode up in the night. Camped in plain view in the meadow on the far side of the old Rawlins cabin. Likely they came in on the trail you all took." He nodded toward me and Jack.

"How many?" said Scribley, squawking his chair back on the wood floor as he stood.

"We counted five, sir."

"Is Dibbs still there?"

"Yes, sir."

"Well . . ." Scribley rubbed his chin. "He's a hotheaded youngster. You'd best ride back there and sit tight. Don't let Dibbs's fiery ways get you in trouble. Do you understand? Do not let those newcomers know you are there."

"Yes, sir." Riley turned to go, but Scribley called him back in.

"Here." He splashed cream in a steaming mug of coffee. "Drink this, warm your insides. Jasper, fix up a sack of food and a canteen of hot water. On second thought, Riley, you stay here, warm up. Neufeld, you're older, Dibbs will listen to you. You ride on out and keep a lid on the situation."

A big blond man stood, nodded, and pulled on his coat.

"We'll all be along soon."

"Yah, yah, yes, sir," said Neufeld. He headed on out the door, stomped down the steps, and was gone.

"Well, that's a new twist in the rope," said Jack, still managing to tuck away bites of bacon and slurps of coffee while everyone else had been listening to Scribley. Jack isn't one to fritter away an opportunity.

True to the rancher's word, we didn't waste time in the

warmth of the dining room. As we filed out the door and headed to the barn, I regretted not being able to tuck into a third helping of flapjacks and coffee. It takes a lot of fuel to fill my firebox, but a good breakfast will go a long way to setting me up for the day.

As we left the room, I was relieved to see that Thomas remained at the table, slowly sipping his coffee and musing on thoughts I am glad to not know.

The morning sun peeked over the ridge behind us, brightening the scrim of frost covering everything. The breaths of all the men plumed, and most rubbed their arms and hands together. Few of them had pulled on coats, hats, and gloves to eat breakfast. The ranch hands split off, hustling their way back to the bunkhouse, a long, low building with smoke puffing out a tidy capped pipe in the center of the shake roof.

Scribley shouted to his men. "Be ready to ride in five minutes." He stayed with me and Jack as we walked to the barn.

As usual, Jack gave voice to my thoughts. "You suppose those newcomers are hired guns of those two in the cabin? Might be they're only passing through."

"There's only one way to find out," I said.

"Yep," said the rancher. "We'll ride in on them and demand answers."

I tamped down a groan. "I was thinking more of spying on them, get a measure of them first."

Scribley stopped, his hand on the handle of the barn door, and looked at me. There was that flint-edge gaze again, for a moment. "Five isn't a whole lot of men," he said.

"True," I said, "unless they're experienced gun hands. Then they're worth two, maybe three times their number."

Maple Jack nodded his agreement. "No offense, Scribley, but me and the boy here, we got experience dealing with hard cases of all sorts. Not saying you don't, but I been a lawman, a scout, a go-between among whites and tribes. Hell, I've held all manner of dicey occupations, and I'm still alive to talk about it. Roamer here is as good as any man I've come up against. You can't prevent us from getting our gear back from those two, nor exacting our revenge from them, neither. So you might as well get used to the notion that we're riding point, and you might as well listen to what we have to say, too."

The creases on the rancher's hard-lined face deepened, then he nodded. "It could be you are right. We'll give them the benefit of the doubt. But they're going to have to work hard to convince me they don't have evil intent."

"No mistake, I'm with you," said Jack. "Now let's get on down there and see what's what."

CHAPTER TWENTY-SEVEN

We were still a half mile from the northern edge of the ranch when we heard the crack of a single gunshot. It pinched off any hopes we had of the five encamped men turning out to be mere travelers. Scribley halted and held up a hand. We all reined up. The men stiffened in their saddles, heads angled, ears cocked. We didn't have long to wait.

Three more shots sounded on the heels of the first. So much for a quick and quiet takeover of the ranch. As we sat there in the roadway, with Scribley's hand still raised, the sound of sudden hooves pounded along the road to our backs. We all spun in our saddles, hands snatching at weapons. It was Thomas, smiling and looking for all the world as if he were heading out on a picnic. The men breathed easier.

Except for me. I was steamed and red-faced. Might be why he hung to the back of the line, well away from me. I'd left him strong instruction to stay put, as had Scribley, by way of offering free run of the house while we were gone. It hadn't mattered what anyone said to Thomas. He behaved as he wanted, as he always did.

Echoes of the last of the shots had not yet faded out before we were thundering down the road, taking no further pains to mask our arrival. We were still a couple of hundred yards from the slight dogleg in the trail that would dump us at the edge of the clearing, close beside the barn. We were greeted by Neufeld, on horseback, shaking his head as he rode up hard. He glanced over his shoulder every few seconds.

"You heard?"

Scribley nodded. "The shots, yes. Where is Dibbs?"

"Yah, dead, I think, sir. I could not stop him. By the time I made it here he had already ridden out and begun himself a shooting match with them. That foolish boy did not make it very far across the meadow."

Scribley gritted his teeth. "Dammit all to hell."

He turned in his saddle. "Riley, Swain, you split the men as you see fit, though I suggest sending men toward the river. I want a group to the east, another along the west edge. Keep to the tree line for cover. We'll do our best to surround them. No shooting unless you have no choice—I want answers before we kill them off. Plenty of time for that later." He turned back, glanced at me. "I brought my rope."

I said nothing, aware Scribley's rage was now justified and personal. I nodded at Jack. "We'll work from the barn toward the house as we can. We're familiar with that route."

Jack grinned. "Yeah, it worked out so nice last time."

"What about me?" It was Thomas, who'd nudged his horse to the front of the line.

"You're going with me," I said, not showing him a smidgen of kindness in my eyes. I wanted to keep the jackass in sight and out of danger.

"No. No, I think not," he said, no doubt sensing my anger. "I'll ride with Mister Scribley."

The rancher offered one curt nod. "Then get to it." He shifted in his saddle, looked at me. "I'll keep an eye on him."

The comment did little to ease my worry about Thomas. He was a greenhorn and the rancher was a thin-skinned brute with a sizable personal ax to grind in the matter. I had no illusions that Scribley would soon forget all else in favor of laying to waste the gunmen and the two inside the house.

"See that you do," I said, and urged Tiny Boy forward, Maple Jack falling in alongside.

"What's the plan, then, Roamer?" he said when we were out of earshot.

"My only ambition is to keep Thomas safe and steal our gear back. The rest of it, Thomas's deed included, is gravy and little consequence to me."

Jack nodded. "Me, I don't want to end up dead like that poor fool kid, Dibbs."

We made it to a cluster of pines adjacent to the barn. From there we saw much of the meadow and, to our left, far off and upslope, two thirds of the log house was visible. Stillness hung over the scene like a sopping quilt.

"Seems we were expected," whispered Jack, sliding from Ol' Mossback. He tied the beast beside Tiny Boy, well within the tree line.

The thick-trunked trees provided decent cover should someone be watching us from the safety of the barn. There were two four-pane glass windows facing us, but frost had clouded them. Good, if we couldn't see in, they weren't seeing out. We drew our revolvers and each quick-peeked around our respective trees.

"How's the shoulder?" asked Jack in a low voice.

"What? You ask me that now?"

Jack chuckled. "Like to know the condition of the folks I'm relying on to save my hide from further perforation."

"Truth be told, I'm amazed at how good it feels, compared with how poor I expect it should feel."

"Answer like that, I may have to think on it some. Why don't you leave off those books and talk like regular folks?"

I ignored him, as I always do when he pretends to look down his nose at what he calls "book learning." Truth is, Jack is as learned as any man I've met. His tall stack of knowledge was

191

gathered and added to from no less a master than life itself. He pays more attention to a day's moments than most folks do to a year's. Then he stuffs each detail into his mind, to be dragged out and used when opportunity arises. It's a simple trait I admire and try to emulate.

"Barn looks safe," I said. "I'm headed over. Cover fire at anything you see flinch—except me."

"Yep."

I did my best to cat foot over to the barn, made it without incident. Then I slid in half-frozen muck right before the barn wall and spun, wrenching my game shoulder and slamming myself back against the building. The noise was impressive.

"You about through?" hissed Jack from the trees.

I waited for an expected fusillade from inside, but heard nothing. I waved Jack over, covering his more dignified stomping run to the other side of the door. The windows flanked us, the double door between us, with the inside single door close to my side.

I reached for the latch, the same one I'd fumbled for in the dark but two nights since, my mind conjuring an unsettling flash of déjà vu. I never got the chance to lift the latch.

We heard a shout to our right, toward the river. Then another shout dissolved into a scream.

"Somebody got a knife to the ribs." Jack bent low and leaned out to peer around the corner of the barn. He was rewarded with a cheek full of splinters and powdered wood as a shot punched through barn boards. "Gaah!" He pawed at his face and his palm came away bloody. "Vicious sons-a-bitches!"

CHAPTER TWENTY-EIGHT

"Can you see?"

He nodded. "Just stung up a little. Now we know they're not set to invite us for tea and cake."

"We also know that scream had to be one of Scribley's men. Likely he blundered in and got himself killed. I'll hope for a better outcome than that for him, but it's not likely."

"Best we can do is learn from his mistake. These five newcomers, if that's all there are, know what they're doing. Until I find out to the contrary, I will assume they're working for the heathens in that shack."

While Jack spoke and picked wood out of his cheek, I risked a peek around the corner closest to me. One quick look, then I pulled my head back. No shots. I bet a second glance wouldn't turn out so lucky. I didn't need one. I had seen what I expected—the humped form of what had to be Dibbs. He looked like someone had dared him to make like a scared turtle, head tucked in and bunched up.

He had been kneeling, then pitched forward, and there he huddled, not moving, in an awkward pose no living man could hold for long. I bet a dollar with myself that the fool kid was dead, at least one shot to the heart or gut, maybe more. It was a stacked bet, as I'd also seen a messy frayed hole, brownish in color, sprouting from the top of his back.

Far to my left, back in the woods but up a ways toward the ridge behind the house, I heard irregular sounds, branches cracking, a quick word then a hushing noise from someone else. If Scribley and his men stomped any louder they might as well break out the brass bugles and play an army ditty.

"Fools," said Jack from behind me. He glanced once back over his shoulder at the shot-up corner. "I'm heading inside." And with that, Jack lifted the latch, and crouching, jumped over the low board at the bottom of the doorway and disappeared into the barn.

I tensed, gritting my teeth. No barrage from waiting gunmen. That was a relief, though I should have been the one to go in first. I made up for it and ducked on in. The smell of the barn was warm and musky and welcoming.

The stable was darker than outdoors, motes drifted in muted shafts of light from the frosted windows. My breath clouded into the same light. I moved my head, quieted my breath, bent low, hugged the wall. "Jack?"

"Yeah, okay."

He hid off to my right, at the open end of the barn, where the buggies and tack were kept. To my left, stalls lined the wall. I heard other breaths, big sounds, horses. A whicker from one, nervous—about us or someone else?

I stood, hugged the wall, angled over along the face of the stalls, one arm out ahead of me. Rounded cribbed wood was splintery beneath my fingertips. No other sounds save for the feathery crunch of my feet in the straw—never quiet. I dropped low once more, some unknown feeling of dread spurred into action by instinct, animal urge to survive, call it what you will, but it's served me well in the past.

Above my head, the whisper of air rushing, something slammed into the stall door, clunking hard and jingling, and knocking my hat to the floor. That same animal instinct drove my arms upward, revolver butt ramming hard into whatever was up there.

I knew somehow it was no horse. But it was a man who was now in an awkward pinch, bent at the waist over the door. My guess was confirmed by a rush of breath followed by a quiet coughing, gagging sound. I smelled coffee, tobacco—a man's breath. My gun butt had not rendered him anything more than dazed, but that was enough.

I clawed at him, my shoulder wound screaming. I figured I'd opened it again, for the fourth or sixth time, who knows? Something under my clothes separated, and a warm wetness leaked down my arm. I didn't care and I didn't stop dragging that ambusher downward.

"Roamer?"

I heard Jack, though was in no spot to reply. The dazed man I struggled with only put up half a fight, but there was something odd about him. What was that clinking sound? Were his arms bound by chains? I stood, dragging him with me, and with a heave launched him backward, arcing through the dim light up and over me. He came down with gathered speed, his back driving down on a saddle rack too hard. I heard a popping sound and it wasn't the wooden rack.

I still had hold of his right arm and his coat, bunched in my fist, in a wad of cloth beside his left ear. He hit the rack and his weak shout of surprise stunted off with a gagging cry. He sagged limp.

As I let go of him and dropped low once more I felt for his wrists, for manacles, but found none. Instead I found a length of logging chain dangling from one fist. He had intended to wrap that chain around my neck. I swallowed, jutted my chin out. I like my neck as it is, stalky, thick, and doing a fine job of holding up my blocky head. And most of all, as yet uncollapsed.

"Roamer!" Jack appeared out of the shadows.

"Yeah, Jack. I'm okay." I jerked my chin. "He isn't."

We peered down at the man.

"His face ain't familiar," said Jack.

"Nor to me." I kept low, scanning the shadowy barn. Jittery horses pawed and nickered, blowing and agitated. They are intelligent creatures, as with most animals, and possess an instinct that humans seem hell-bent on carving away from ourselves.

They smelled the man's death. As to that, so did I. His innards had let go and the sudden stink of his leavings mingled with the rank tang of blood and urine layered atop the dusty barn smell. When this was over I would open this barn wide and get these animals outside. But not yet.

Jack checked for a heartbeat, though I knew it wasn't possible. The man's back had snapped with a final sound that left no doubt. I've laid a few men low and never once, not even with the foulest, most deserving of them, did I take pleasure in the deed.

"Well, he had it coming," said Jack, pawing the man's waist for his gun rig. He unbuckled it and held it up to me. I shook my head. My waist was bigger than most and the man was slender. Jack strapped it on beneath his paunch, grunting it into place. "Any other scurvy, rotten devils in here?" he said in a bolder, louder voice.

No response, not that we expected one. But if there had been only five hired men, that left four, not counting any prisoners Scribley and his men may have taken, though on that score I was not hopeful. It felt as if we were making no progress at all in this frustrating venture, as if we were wading through waist-deep snow in the middle of a blizzard.

Jack made a few more scuffling, grunting sounds, and emerged out of the shadows to my right. "Nothing over there," he whispered, "except dust, an old barouche, and a work wagon with no wheels."

"Unless the rest of these stalls hold critters other than horses,

I'd say we're safe." As I said it I stepped like a hefty toe dancer along the front of the stalls, peering in from the corners. There were still ample shadows for them to hide in should someone else be in there, but it was doubtful. Being only five strong, they likely wouldn't post more than a single man in the barn.

Shots cracked, thin and quick, from down by the river.

"Sounds like something's cooking," said Jack. "Come on, we've already dallied in here long enough. We have to get to that house."

"That's the problem, it's open all around it."

"I know," he said, "but we knew that before."

"And we didn't have a plan then, either."

"Back to back?"

I nodded, but then had an idea. "Help me with this stall door. It should be thick enough."

"Shield?"

"Yep."

The end stall was empty, and I swung the door open. It was four feet wide and maybe five tall. The steel strap hinges were loose and the door fit oddly, sagging as it creaked open. I slipped inside the stall. It was darker in there, smelled dusty, and there was little on the floor save for dirt and dents from some horse's feet of years before.

"Close it," I told Jack. "Then stand away." I drove the flat of my boot bottom, heel first, at the spot the top hinge sat. The blow echoed, whomped, echoed again, kick after kick, six or so, but it was paying off.

"Roamer, you'll tucker yourself out before we get started!"

I said nothing but gave it one more go and the top hinge splintered free, sagging the door. The bottom hinge was quick work, and in another few seconds we had our shield.

We must have looked like a comedic stage troupe with elaborate props as we sidled out of the barn and made our slow way toward the house. The door's original strap-leather handle gave me a suitable grip to carry it by.

I held the door up in front of us, my revolver, gripped in my weaker arm, cocked and ready. His back to mine, Jack walked tight against me, a gun in each hand. In this manner we made our way across the span of meadow toward the house. I stuck to the worn path, as there was no reason not to. It's not as if we were taking pains to hide ourselves.

Soon enough the door proved its worth and justified the trouble of dismantling it. I heard glass shattering, then shots seared in from the house, plunking into the wood. Two more furrowed dirt before me. They were trying to shoot my feet, which were visible when I stepped. There was no way I could hunch lower and still shuffle forward.

Other shots whistled in. I saw puffs of smoke from along the river indicating where the shots came from.

"Hey, now! Hey!" Jack barked those and other cackling sounds as he cranked off shots to either side of us, then a few over my head toward the house. The man is talkative, even in grim situations. In this manner we made our slow way to the log house. I wanted to get close enough to hug the outer wall, then decipher a way in from there.

There wasn't nearly as much gunfire from our flanks or rear as I expected. Even Jack seemed disappointed. "Where in the hell did everybody go?"

"Don't fret," I said. "Bound to be more than the two of them in the house."

"Look at that!" said Jack, nodding toward the meadow beyond the house.

I shifted the door and peeked. Three of Scribley's men, on foot, with the rancher himself close behind, chased a limping man across the brown grass. Shots barked, whistled by, then one of the men shouted to the others and made way for Scribley, who ran well for his age.

He pushed past his men and jerked to a stop, shouldered a shotgun, and triggered one barrel, then the second. The first caught the pursued man high on the shoulders, pitched him forward. The second sliced into his legs as they whipped upward from the impact of the first blast. It was vicious and final, and horrific to witness.

More shots echoed from the river, this time not at us but toward the rancher and his men. I didn't see Thomas among them and hoped Scribley had given him a stern talking to and left him back in the woods. We were still out in the middle of the action with our drawers down and flapping.

"Let's pick up the pace," I said.

"Waitin' on you, boy!" Jack ripped off another shot toward the tree line by the river.

"You see somebody?"

"Nope, just lettin' 'em know Maple Jack's still dancing!"

Three strides closer—we were about sixty feet from the foremost corner of the house—and two rifles opened up on us. The stall door rattled and pinged as bullets chewed their way into the shredding planks. We were close enough now that they began making their way through the wood. I jammed the door to the grass and we crouched lower, waiting out the barrage, not keeping too close to the wood erupting in finger-size holes before us.

CHAPTER TWENTY-NINE

"Can't take much more of this," said Jack.

"When they stop to reload, let's rush it."

"Lead the way," said Jack with a grin.

And that's what we did, right up to the house. We hugged it close, too close for those in the house to crank off a decent shot at us without leaning out the windows. I didn't think they'd do that, for then they would be easy targets themselves.

Far down the meadow, one of the strangers had his back pinned against one of those fancy fences, trapped like a mountain lion cornered in a box canyon. Must have been the man who had been hiding along the river, likely the one who had taken a shot at Jack and splintered his face up.

The man had visible wounds, and no visible guns. And Scribley and his boys closed in fast. They stopped about six feet from him, three of the four ranch hands held drawn, aimed revolvers, the fourth a rifle. As before, Scribley walked up behind them, another of his men behind him.

I didn't know as I had an accurate count of how many men he had, but I seem to recall seeing nine, ten with the rancher himself. That left half of his men elsewhere. Maybe still up above the cabin in the woods. From that distance, none that I could see looked like Thomas.

And in the next instant I saw why. Shots cracked from within the house. Though Jack and I hugged the log wall of the cabin, we flinched, trying to look in every direction at once, up toward the windows and to our sides, each expecting to see a smoking barrel and to feel smacking pain as our blood leaked out. But no, Jack nudged me in the gut and nodded upslope behind the cabin.

There came Thomas. Two emotions, raw terror and unbridled glee, warred on his face as he bounded spring-legged down the slope toward us.

He clutched a rifle around the forestock with one flailing arm, and nearly somersaulted, so wildly was he leaping. Then he locked his gaze on us. His foolish grin widened, as did his terror-round eyes, and a bullet whipped the hat off his head as if cuffed from behind by a trickster's hand.

Thomas slid to a stop, spraying gravel and unearthing clumps of dried grass. Most astounding of everything I'd seen already that day, the young fool scrabbled back upslope to retrieve his hat.

"Thomas!" I shouted, peeling away from the wall. Jack knew what I was up to and kept to his spot, but harangued the foolish young man with a volley of words I don't dare repeat.

Jack sent three bullets at the rear-most window at our end of the house. I gulped, dry-mouthed, and prayed the distraction would prevent whoever was shooting at the boy from getting off another shot.

Trouble was, the new commotion mystified Thomas as well. He spun and stood still on the slope, his fallen hat in one hand, halfway to his head, mouth agape.

"Get down here!" I bellowed. And when I do that, which isn't often, it usually commands immediate attention. This time was no different. Thomas ran. Rock chips spattered where his right foot had been a second before. That time he did lose his footing, and that is likely what saved him, for he rolled like a pushed boulder right down before Jack's feet.

And that's where we stayed put for longer than I care to

201

relate. It was mid-morning by that time and the blue strafings of sky that earlier promised a fine day had been blotted out by clouds, low and driving in lower, dark and filled with gloom.

We stood there, the three of us, huddled and hugging the wall for the next few minutes, trying to be quiet, or rather trying to keep Thomas quiet. I had the added task of keeping Jack from thumping Thomas on the head.

"I can't take much more of this," said Jack. "We have to do something. Even if it's wrong. Time to make a move."

Thomas was about to open his yap, but I held up a finger and shook my head. I felt the veins pulsing on my temples, knew my brushy face, now more than a week since I'd shaved, looked worse than before, and that's saying something.

I was not up for hearing Thomas's voice whining like a late-night mosquito in my ears. A close second would be to hear him spout orders in his imperious rich-boy's voice. So far he'd taken the hint and kept his mouth shut. But it wouldn't last, with him it never did.

"I'm headed around the front, Jack," I said in a whisper. "You take the back, we'll meet up on the far side, see if we can tell how many are in there. At least two, as the shots overlapped. Might be we'll figure out a way for one of us to distract them, enough for the other to climb the stairs, kick in the door, and settle this mess once and for all."

"Good, let's go." With a quick glance upward toward the windows, one of them now shattered from the shots I'd cranked in, he crept low to the corner.

I did the same. I stopped, pointed again at Thomas and mouthed, "Stay put!" He stared at me as though he found my obvious rage confounding. I've been acquainted with feral wolf dogs with better abilities to mind.

As I feared, the front and two ends of the house were closed up tighter than a bank vault. The door I'd so recently scrambled out of when rescuing Thomas stood six or so steps up to a landing. From there it wrapped around and became the setting porch along the front of the place. The door had been cobbled back into shape after the woman had blasted it with the shotgun. Nothing for it, I'd have to go on up there and barge in somehow.

I crept back around to where we'd started, hoping Jack had learned of a way in, maybe a back door—wishful, fanciful thinking, but it pays to explore all potential options before barging in on a dicey setup.

I slipped around the corner and there was Jack, making his way around back, but no sign of Thomas. We exchanged raised-eyebrow glances and then we heard someone whisper, "Hey!"

We looked upward.

There was Thomas, at the top of the stairs, crouched down and grinning at us. His rifle was not in his hands. He'd left it leaning against the logs beside us.

We both groaned.

"Keep your head down, you fool!" hissed Jack.

"Cover me," I said and made my way up the stairs, one at a time, wincing with each creak and pop of the planking.

I made it up there without attracting any shots my way, but when I got to the top, that damned Thomas had wormed his way around to the front. I followed and found him laid out prone, inching his head up close to the bottom of the nearest window. It was shuttered, likely barred from the inside.

I wasn't about to shout, but I wanted to lay a hand on him and drag him back off there. Hell, if I'm honest I wanted to grab him by a leg and toss him off the porch to the ground below.

Instead, I heard voices inside. A man's first, rapid. His words sounded like questions, as if he were pleading with someone.

I stood, looked in a gap between the shutter and the window itself, at the side of the same window Thomas was perched beneath. An oil lamp's low glow made visible little of the interior.

A shape passed before the lamp, then moved back. Was it the man, the woman, or a third person—one of the men who'd arrived overnight? That's when an unsettling thought occurred to me once more—what if these five men really were just passing through? The last I'd seen of any of the newcomers, they were being hunted down by Scribley and his crew and shot like hydrophobic wolves.

What if they were innocent, had only wanted a place to camp for the night? What if Dibbs had somehow goaded them into a gunfight? Hell, what if Dibbs had been shot by this lot in the house? Worrisome notions, though nothing in this vein of thought accounted for the attack by the man in the barn.

As with much in this life, the more complicated the situation became, the more seductive the simple solutions, such as those the hot-headed rancher was employing. I hoped for all our sakes the newcomers had been in league with these two gems inside the cabin. Otherwise, we were all answerable for far more deaths and damage than we'd been dealt by them.

The man's voice inside was trampled by a woman's. Hers was low, husky, a barking sound. The man's voice wedged in, timid, nipping, yapping something, then retreating as if afraid of getting smacked.

"We can still make money," he said. "Sell off the land once we get out of here."

"You idiot, you think we're getting out of here?" said the woman. She followed it with a spitting sound, accentuating the truth of her suspicions.

A clinking sounded, then the woman said, "Don't be stingy. Pour me another!"

The man grumbled, and she said, "What? What was that?"

"Nothing, dearest."

"Dearest, ha. You hate me." Her voice was loud, though the

words slurred. A few seconds later something hit the wall close by the window I'd been looking through.

"Don't care." It was the man's voice. "You said it was good mining land, but it don't matter. We can sell off this ranch, make a pile, and no one's the wiser. Have to get to the coast."

She responded, but he cut her off. I didn't think she'd take that well. I was right. Her reverie ended with a shriek. "Two thousand acres! I'm not giving it away!"

That raised my eyebrows. I looked down at Thomas, who shrugged, his weak smile saying all his voice hadn't. The property was larger than he let on. I assumed that was intentional on his part. Yep, I thought. As oily as his father.

I say *his* because I will never admit that Italian scoundrel was my father. Of course, knowing what I did of my mother, it was as likely someone else had fathered me. The thought did not depress me. It was something I'd dreamt of as a youth, and I came to the same solution then as now—I did not care. I'm alive, here and now, and that's what mattered. Does a wolf or a grizzly or a diamondback or a saguaro cactus fret about who or what begat it?

Not having ever been one of any of those, or any critter other than a human, I can't say for certain. But a solid guess is . . . no. So why should I? If I've learned anything trailing after Maple Jack all these years (and he would argue I have learned little), it's that people as a rule dwell far too much in their minds on notions they cannot change. We would do well to behave more as animals do.

In my experience, most critters, other than humans, live from moment to moment, feeding when they are hungry and backing away from the dinner table when they are not. They fight when threatened, and laze in the sun when no danger is close by. This notion has long struck me as sound and I strive to live in such a manner. Not so with the shouting folks in the cabin.

CHAPTER THIRTY

Back inside, the couple went at it again, hammer and tongs, and shouts ripped from both of them. Something told me calmer language was no thing they would ever utter.

The ruckus was sounding better all the time to me, and I pressed my face closer to the gap in the board to see if they were alone and armed. That's when Thomas chose to utter a loud whimper. He'd propped himself up on a knee beside me. The noises inside pinched off like a blown match, then the lamp was blown out.

I heard frantic whisperings, something dragged across the floor, came closer to the window. I backed away from my spot, but kept the revolver thumbed back and ready. I was about to bend down and grab Thomas by the ankle when a shot from inside crashed into the shutters. They blew outward, ripped clean of half their weight in wood.

I had hoped that the drunken couple might well do themselves in, deal mutual mortal blows, and, luck of luck, save us the headache of doing it ourselves. I hoped so, anyway.

Now, thanks to Thomas, we were exposed, and there was only one direction this mess could run—straight into a fusillade.

I clapped a hand down hard onto his shoulder, at the same time heard a yelp from Jack down below.

Nothing to lose at this point, I knee-walked backward, dragging the fool boy with me, and shouted quickly to Jack: "We're good!"

No response from him, so I knew he took it in stride and was likely moving around back to figure a way into the house.

I wasn't able to look in two directions at once, still not, in fact, and the lack of that ability is what nearly got me killed. Yet of all wonders, Thomas saved me. I'd like to say I was happy about it, but it still bothers me. Childish, but there you have it.

Though I was dragging him backward toward a safe stretch of wall, Thomas, who was still facing the window where we'd been snooping, shouted, "Scorfano!" as the brute end of a shotgun poked out. It was leveled at me, a foot above Thomas's head, and barked flame.

I had enough time to twist out of the path of certain death, though I felt the whistling of the buckshot as the pellets sliced air by my head. If Thomas hadn't shouted, I would have caught the blast full in the face.

I finished dragging him and slammed him, out of harm, against the logs.

The proceedings were not going as I had planned. For a pair of angry drunks, the man and woman certainly were formidable foes. I looked out across the meadow, but saw no sign of Scribley and his boys. I did see a man leaning against the plank fencing, his arms draped across the topmost board, his head bent all the way back as if he were enjoying a few quiet moments in the sun.

But the rest of him told the story. His white shirt beneath a brown wool coat, parted in the center, was a splotchy, mud-red mess. He was dead, or on his way there. Gut-shot men rarely do well. Most often it's a slow, certain trail to death. How he remained upright was a mystery.

I wondered where Jack had gotten to, but didn't dare open my mouth. After the hollow clash of the shotgun blast ebbed away, and with ears ringing like a town crier's bell, I noticed the fullness of the silence that had draped over the scene. It lasted for a number of seconds, then I heard footsteps inside the house once more. A bottle clinked against a glass.

"Too much, I tell you!" The man's voice was reedy, shrieking. "Too much shooting and killing! The filching I can swallow, but all this shooting and killing and hiring others to do your foul deeds! You got—"

She cut him off fast, hard, and with a finality that marked her for who she was—a ruthless woman. "Shut that drunken mouth of yours. You think I can wait for you to make us rich? Up to you we'd be all but naked, gibbering in the gutter for bread and water."

He said something else, but again she stomped all over his words until he simmered once more. "You don't shut your mouth you will regret it mighty, I tell you." Her voice was a mannish growl.

Another clink, then a thump as the glass was set on a hard surface. "You ain't got it in you, you foul hog. I could have had a different life, taken over the folks' home place back in Ohio. Now look at me! I have wasted my life with you and I am done, finished, all over it now."

I heard bootsteps cross the room, then the sound of someone from within wrestling with the poorly repaired door. It raised up a couple of inches and jerked inward.

With no more warning and no more words from inside, the man emerged. As soon as I saw the side of his head I knew there was no way I could shoot him. He was unarmed, drunk, and well on his way to being unable to walk. He crossed the few feet to the steps, and miraculously worked his way down them to the ground. Where was Jack? He should be down there, making sure the old man didn't run for it.

The drunk hit the grass, stayed upright, tottering slowly along the pathway toward the barn. "I want a truce! Keep me free and away from this bitch. She's evil, you all know it! Hell, we've left a trail of dead bodies and stolen goods all the way from Ohio. Finally get us a cozy cabin where we can take 'er easy, enjoy the fruit of our work. But no, not this one!"

He thrust a skinny arm roughly back over his shoulder, pointed at the house. Then he turned, faced the house, and shouted. "You witch! You evil cur! The Good Lord has saw fit to kill off most of your mean-eyed kin, but not you! You take everything and then some. Take take ta—"

The crack of a rifle shot echoed through the window to my right and the bullet whipped straight into the man's head, up above the eyes. It cored a path clean and true, and looked for a moment like a third eye. Then blood bubbled out, leaked down his face.

A second shot drove him to his knees, already dead. His arms flung straight out to the sides and he pitched facedown. His bald head smacked a rock like a hand slapping water.

Beside me Thomas threw up. I rolled my eyes and left him there. Time was precious. I peered around the corner once more hoping to snatch up the end of the rifle. But the burly cow of a woman had already withdrawn it. I gave Thomas one more silent admonition then kept on, edging toward the still-open door. I swallowed hard once and held the revolver at full cock, poised before me. As I stepped into the doorway, I did what I could to make myself a small target. Wishful thinking.

I didn't pause there but dropped low and clambered on in. I had to end this right now, she was too crazy, shooting her own man, likely her husband.

The room was darkened from lack of lamplight, for the closed shutters, and for the clouded day's wan light. But I didn't see her in there. Back in the next room, then. The door was closed. She would be in there with her rifle, shotgun, or both, waiting to finally deal me the blow she'd been trying for many days now to deliver.

By then I'd had more than my fill of this foul, hellish creature and her unending shenanigans. My shoulder was a clot of pain that exploded like lightning with each step I took. My energy dwindled, and what little patience I had left me when she shot that wretched drunk.

I moved straight at that closed door to the inner room, raising my revolver and glancing quickly to make sure I had reloaded. I had.

I did not stop, but raised a boot high and drove the sole hard at the wooden latch. The entire door shuddered, cracked in half lengthwise, and spasmed inward. As soon as I felt the door giving way beneath my boot I turned sideways and followed it on in, hugging tight to the right side of the frame.

My shirt snagged on something, a jutting knot or a nail, and tore. I kept going, and made it out of the doorway in time to see a shotgun blast from the middle of the room savage the doorway. A couple of pellets nibbled at me, but I was still on the move, unsure if she was about to trigger the second barrel. She didn't. She threw the spent shotgun at me. What she did with her rifle I had no idea. At least it wasn't in her hands.

I barreled straight at her as I had the door, and she squealed, actually squealed, like a barnyard pig chased by a hound.

The room was dim, the only light coming from the front window she'd blasted out, the same one I'd peeked in not long before. It overlooked the porch and I found myself hoping someone might lean inside the frame, to lend a hand and an extra barrel so we could stop this pig of a woman from trampling around the small room. Her breathing was ragged, her wheezing squeals louder and more frantic with each odd maneuver she made.

She hurled herself onto a bed, the frame groaning as she

rolled. I figured all I had to do was wait her out, keep her from bolting out the door, through the kitchen, and down the stairs. Even at that she'd come to some end. With Jack and Scribley and his men outside, there was no way she could make an escape. They'd all witnessed the mess she'd dealt her partner, the drunk. She was done for, regardless.

She bounced off the bed, snatching up spare, dusty furnishings and whipping them in my direction: an oil lamp that shattered against the back wall, a woman's fancy hat which I recognized as the one she'd worn on the street in Forsaken, a hairbrush, and lastly a small ladder-back chair.

She surprised me yet again with her agility by bolting straight for that blasted-out front window. Like a fat rabbit through a hole in a fence, she dove on through, headfirst, and landed on the porch floor. I made for the window myself, and that's when Thomas appeared.

He nearly fell over her, surprised to see the hog flop at his feet. The oddness of the moment stunned all three of us, but Thomas broke the spell. He grabbed her by the snaky nest of silver-and-red hair atop her head and shoved a revolver in her snout. "Stop this madness, damn you! Stop it now, I say!"

And she did.

"Get on your feet!"

And she did.

I headed for the window to lend him a hand.

And then she raked his face with the talon-like nails of her fat right hand, snatching away the revolver with her left. She was fast, fast enough to turn the gun on him, jamming it into his cheek hard enough that it pushed his head to the side. His thin face puckered around the barrel.

I moved forward, nearly to the window, hoping to get in a quick shot. She wrapped an arm around his neck and yanked him down to her height, jamming the barrel harder into his face. Any boldness Thomas had shown moments before drizzled down his trouser leg. He simpered and blubbered. Tears oozed out his eyes, snot strung from his nose.

"Shut up! Shut your mouth!"

He tried, and managed to reduce his display of fear to a moan and a few shallow breaths.

The piggy woman was at a momentary loss as to what to do next. If she headed toward the steps, she would expose her back to me. If she backed toward the steps, she would expose herself from the rear to whoever might be waiting at the end of the porch, around the corner. I hoped it was Jack.

I had no clear shot from my angle. I'd advanced too far to one side and now once more she had the upper hand. As long as she didn't carry through with her threat and shoot Thomas, I didn't care. If I didn't rile her she might well leave Thomas alive.

That was the weak-kneed, logical way around the tree.

What I did instead was inch my way forward to better position myself to shoot her at the first possible moment. And that's when everything changed.

A tremendous burst of rupturing glass filled the air in the dark to my left. The shattered window panes blew inward, pushed from the outside by the wood shutters that had covered them. The wood popped and snapped. I saw a burly hand grab one canted ruptured board, wrench it backward quickly. Jack. I'd know those clamp-like hands and that ragged buckskin cuff anywhere. Twice more and he'd cleared enough wood to climb through.

"Get him out of there! Back out!" The fat woman's shouts had grown more frantic, frazzle-edged.

Her threats didn't stop Jack. He grunted on in through that ragged back window and made his way straight across the room. When he was but a few feet from the window she'd jumped through, she screamed again.

"Stop where you are or I'll shoot this fool in the head!"

That dragged a whole new round of moans and racking sobs from Thomas. She jammed the barrel harder than ever into his face and growled something at him.

Jack dropped to his knees with a pop and a grunt, and leveled his old war cannon up through the ragged window hole, directly on her. "Let the boy be, you evil sow."

Jack's voice was smooth and level. I knew what he had in mind and I stopped my advance toward her.

"Thomas!" I shouted and he skittered his eyes at me.

"Don't talk to him!" squealed the pig woman.

"Thomas, step away . . . now!"

As soon as I sent that last word out of my mouth, Jack's shot cored the harpy's forehead. For once, Thomas did as I said, and in quick fashion, too. The brute of a woman collapsed backward, crashing through the porch railing, snapping the top rail under her girth. She kept on going, eight or so feet down to the ground, and slopped in a grotesque heap.

Jack and I climbed through the window and joined Thomas in looking down at her. She'd landed partially on her head, not that it mattered—Jack's shot was true and final. The man can shoot. But it was not a pretty scene. The fall snapped her neck, canted the head too far to one side, her mouth wide, as if she were trying to gnaw at her own shoulder. A ragged halo of blood leached into the brittle brown grass.

Her dress, a much-mended blue-and-white garment, had split and the thick body she'd stuffed into it that morning sagged out the side. One arm was trapped beneath her girth.

"That's for the girl," Jack said in a near whisper. "And for filching my prize lynx hat." He turned and walked down the length of the porch.

CHAPTER THIRTY-ONE

By the time we made it to her, Scribley and his men had closed in. We looked down at the sloppy wreck of a woman for a few moments, no one certain what to say or do next.

The rancher shifted to the crook of his right arm the shotgun he was carrying, and broke the silence. He looked up at Jack, then at me and Thomas, and grinned. The first time he'd done that in a long while, I'll wager. "Well done, men." He offered a hand. "Well done. You have my congratulations."

You could have punched Jack in the face and pleased him more. The old mountain man stepped backward as if Scribley had offered him a handful of fresh dog leavings, and turned away.

It didn't affect the rancher. He turned his attention back to the woman. Next we saw, he'd dropped to his knees beside her, jamming the butt of the shotgun to the ground, using it as a prop. Before we could stop him, he pawed at her breasts with his free hand.

"See here, Scribley," growled Jack. "That ain't right!"

The rancher ignored him and shouted, "Ha! Ha!" He held aloft a wrinkled, bloodstained wad of folded papers. "The deed! The deed! At long last, I have the deed!" He stood, holding it tight in his left hand, and walked away staring at it. "Oh, praise God."

Scribley didn't seem to notice as Jack stepped before him and put a hand to the rancher's shoulder. "Easy now, Scribley."

Jack's voice was kind but firm, as if he were speaking to a child who'd unknowingly stepped out of line. "That belongs to the boy, to Thomas over there. That's why we're all here, ain't it?"

Scribley reacted as if slapped. "But this was stolen from me!" He backed away, looking at us all, me, Jack, Thomas, his own men. "Cover me, boys. Don't let them at me!" This last he directed to his ranch hands, but they stood still, looking confused and weary from the day's dark undertakings.

"Damn you all to hell!" Scribley barked the words and kept walking toward the barn and the lane beyond, where the horses were tied along the tree line.

Jack, Thomas, and I followed, with Scribley's men thronging close. I tried to crack this odd new shell the rancher had covered himself with. "Mister Scribley, this isn't the way. That deed rightfully belongs to Thomas. You're no better than those who stole it from him."

For a moment I thought perhaps I'd gotten to him, but he barely paused before stepping up his pace. As he strode, more purposefully with each step, it seemed as if he had made some decision, as if his former forthright attitude was taking over once more.

I wasn't certain what was about to happen, but I saw Jack had the same thought as me—he rested a gnarled hand on the butt of his Dragoon. In case the situation dug itself further down the dank hole it was headed.

Scribley walked to the nearest of the assembled mounts tied off by the pines. Standing smack-dab between Tiny Boy and Ol' Mossback the mule, Scribley turned and faced us. Once more he wore the odd, beaming smile. He tucked the deed into an inner coat pocket, looked at his men, all of whom ringed us, and said, "Kill them."

"What?" said Thomas, backing up, his hands raised before him as if he could shove the bad situation backward.

"Those three are as I suspected from the first, nothing more than common thieves. I am the law in these parts and I order you to kill them."

CHAPTER THIRTY-TWO

A raven rasped by high above. Everyone who had a weapon drew it, though no one knew quite where to aim. Scribley's smile melted once more into a mask of intolerance and bubbling rage. His cheeks reddened and I swore I heard his teeth grind together.

He raised the scattergun he'd kept cradled in the crook of his right arm, and brought it to bear up high, snugged to his right shoulder.

"Hey now!" shouted Jack, his ancient revolver poised in a firm grip. "Enough of this!"

But Scribley didn't hear him. He was too busy leveling that shotgun first at one then another of us. "I said kill them! Now, damn you!"

His men might not have known what to do, but at least they weren't following his orders. Then Neufeld, the big Swede, said, "No . . ." He swallowed, licked his lips, began speaking again. "No, sir! We will kill no more for you. It is not right . . . sir!"

Swain stepped forward, his repeater held gut high, aimed in Scribley's general direction. He nodded. "Neufeld's right sir. No more killing. It's . . . it's too much."

A strangled bark of rage flew from Scribley's mouth. "You weak-souled bastards! After all I've done for you!" He snugged the shotgun tight to his shoulder, even as shouts came from us all.

But quick as the angry rancher was, the mighty Percheron,

Tiny Boy, was quicker. And annoyed at all the commotion so close to his head. His demeanor is dicey on his best days, and the past week hadn't helped his disposition any. He drove that big head of his downward, nostrils wide, and quick as a bee sting sank teeth into Scribley's shoulder.

The rancher howled, saved from severe damage by his thick coat. He jumped to the side, and swung that heavy shogun upward. The barrels caught Tiny alongside the jaw. I heard it smack and saw the big horse flinch, jerk his head to one side.

"No!" I shouted, certain the fool rancher was going to shoot my horse. The angle was all wrong, and Scribley backed up fast to make it right.

I bolted forward, but Neufeld was already ahead of me.

"Drop it now, Mister Scribley! We have had enough of this!"

Reason filled the silence. Scribley relaxed, slowly lowered the shotgun, and let it drop to the ground. He turned toward us, a drained look on his face. I saw blood leaking down the fingertips of his right hand, dripping onto his boot. Tiny Boy had landed a solid bite after all.

Scribley nodded slowly, as if finally taking in Neufeld's demand. His eyes rose, focused on us. He stood up straight. Then faster than I could have imagined, the surly rancher dragged upward with his good hand, raking free a revolver from its holster.

He thumbed back on the hammer as Neufeld, Swain, me, Jack, and everyone else shouted, "No!" once more.

Gunshots barked.

Scribley's thick body jerked left, then right with each plowing blow. He convulsed forward as he dropped, as if sledged, to his knees. He dropped the revolver and looked down at his chest. With bloody, shaking hands he reached into his coat and pulled out the deed, now little more than a mass of bloodied, shredded paper. He stared at it, horror widening his red eyes.

He looked outward, as if through us all, toward the meadow, his trembling fingers groping the air before him. "My . . . land!"

His eyes rolled heavenward, then he pitched face-first to the ground. A long, slow wheeze drained out of him and his hands and feet, shoulders and head all sagged as they gave up their tasks for the last time, not in sleep but in death.

CHAPTER THIRTY-THREE

Over the next couple of hours, the ranch hands faced the mess they'd created that day—a mess I am ashamed to say we brought to their doorstep, though Jack disagrees. One by one they told us, as if in a defensive eulogy, what a good man Clement Scribley really was. He was a hard man, they said, but always fair in his treatment of them. And if his handling of strangers appeared harsh, it nearly always proved, in the end, to ring with truth, no matter how bitter the tolling sounded.

As the years passed, though, his belief that strangers were not to be trusted warped to become a conviction that all strangers were criminals. So when we three happened along, the men were surprised he didn't bull ahead and try to string us up. They figured he intended to keep us alive long enough to glean information about the neighboring ranch, then kill us off when it suited him.

Looking back on the day before, we were worn out, to be sure, but we should have been more wary. He lulled us into trusting him with that damn tasty venison stew. But that's neither here nor there, as we lived through it.

"Too bad about the five strangers who rode in, though." My comment was sincere, but it raised the ire of Neufeld.

"What do you mean?" His big Scandinavian jaw jutted. "They were hired killers, yah? That much was plain."

"Was it now?" said Jack, crossing his arms, the Maple Jack equivalent to jutting his jaw. " 'Cause they could just as easy have been innocents riding on through. Bad luck on them that they showed when they did, got cornered here."

Swain toed the dirt, looked red in the face. "Now, we don't know that."

"You're right, young fella. We don't. Nor do we have any such proof that Scribley was right, neither."

Swain perked up, pointed a finger. "There was Dibbs, though. They shot him."

"Did they?" I said, joining the fray. "Could have been the folks at the house. None of us was here when Dibbs was shot, after all."

Murmurs of begrudging agreement rippled through the small group.

Of course, none of this palaver explained the man in the barn. If they were innocents, it's likely he was afraid for his life, logical if those in the house were the ones doing the shooting. None of it sat well with me.

"We'll likely never know," said Jack. "What's done is done. Law will have to be called in to poke and prod the situation." He looked around at the desolate place, a ranch that but two days before had seemed so pretty and promising. "They won't figure it out neither, I expect."

"I will send men to ride for the law in Walla Walla," said Neufeld.

Jack and I nodded. Up to then, Thomas had been silent. For all the day had brought him, a city boy from back East with frail sensibilities, I could hardly blame him. To my surprise, he cleared his throat and looked around at the gathered men. "For what it is worth to you all, I am sorry, truly sorry, to have brought this"—he gestured broadly with outstretched hands—"this mess to your door."

His words seemed genuine, and the men appeared to take them in the way they were intended. There was something about him that made me want to believe his budding sincerity. I was wary, though, as throughout this venture he'd made a habit of pulling the rug out from under me. Maybe the day's raw proceedings had changed him.

"Since he had no heirs, what do you suppose will become of the ranch?" said Jack later, as we stood by Neufeld watching the buckboard carrying Scribley and Dibbs back to the home ranch.

The big blond man turned a quizzical look on Jack. "What do you mean?"

"He confided to us he was a bachelor, hadn't found the right woman yet. Hopin', he was. Like the rest of us. Hope is eternal, but can be a mighty poor substitute for companionship."

I marveled not for the first time at Maple Jack's propensity for doling out satisfying helpings of wisdom. He'd given me much to chew on over the years and I reckon he will for some time to come, Lord willing.

"No, no, Mister Scribley was no bachelor. At least not as you say. He was, how do you say it, putting you on, yah? He had a wife, yes." He nodded at our confused looks. "But she died years ago. She worked herself to death to please him. But what took her in the end was a broken heart. When their daughter left home."

"Daughter?" I said, my mind working over our extensive conversation with Scribley, wondering if anything he had told us was the truth.

"Yah, she could not stand his harsh ways. I think she is the one who will inherit it all now." He sighed, looked suddenly so sad. "She was a beautiful girl, such pretty green eyes."

Now it was Jack's turn at surprise. Even in the waning light of that cold autumn afternoon I saw the high color drain from his face. "What was she like?" His question came out as little more than a whisper.

Neufeld nearly smiled then, lost in fond recollection. "Bold she was, and with a laugh as if she had no cares. But she was more like her mother, a good soul. Though enough of her father in her to be always at odds with him. That is what made her leave, I think." He nodded again, looking as though he were holding back tears.

Jack shook his head slowly and closed his eyes.

I could do nothing but stare at my big, dumb boots. It had to be her.

It was Thomas who spoke, surprising me once more. "What was her name?"

"Carla," said Neufeld. "Her name is Carla."

Thomas rubbed his fingers hard in his eyes. He looked for all the world as he did when he was five and caught by Mimsy with the pasty remnants of one of her berry pies on his hands and cheeks.

"What is all this?" said Neufeld. He squared off on us. "What do you know?"

I sighed. "She was on her way back here. We knew her for a time. On the trail. She was as you say, kind."

Neufeld nearly smiled, but caught himself, caution edging his voice. "What do you know? What are you not telling me?"

"She was murdered by a man. He . . . he was working for those two in the house. We buried her there, not many days back."

A low groan escaped the big blond man's mouth. "And her killer?" he whispered, finally, his face and voice hollowed, gaunt.

"We done for him," said Jack, sounding like he was speaking through gravel. "We avenged her."

The big ranch foreman didn't say anything. For long moments the only sound was Thomas's quiet crying. Then Neufeld breathed deeply. "I will bring her back here, to be buried with her mother . . . and father."

He said nothing more, but handed Thomas the bloodied,

bullet-riddled deed. Then he mounted his horse as if he were a hundred years old. We watched him ride slowly out of sight.

CHAPTER THIRTY-FOUR

We spent the next couple of days burying the dead, assembling what personal effects as we could find off their bodies and among their traps. This we saved for the law. While we waited, we tidied and repaired broken doors and windows as best we could.

After three days, two lawmen from Walla Walla showed up and did their best to sort through the mess of a story we told them. They left, more confused than when they arrived.

We were relieved that they seemed convinced of our innocence. But we know we are guilty of so much in this messy episode. It will be long days of quiet pondering before I sort out what I did and what I should have done better. If I am a harsh taskmaster, Maple Jack is a brutal dictator when judging himself. He may never forgive himself for his part in this. I am not certain how Thomas will fare. He remained tight-mouthed, working alongside us as I'd never seen him.

The lawmen backtracked to Scribley's place, and I later found out no one there was on the hook for breaking any laws. I suspect it was set down in the logbooks as a sad mess all around.

We'd also told the lawmen of Scribley's daughter, of the location of her grave, and of the grave of the man who'd killed her. Scribley's men said they'd check with Neufeld to make certain he brought her body back. I didn't think he needed reminding. His sad face still comes to mind at times.

I wonder if he loved the girl, wonder if he thought of her

every day when she was gone. If he hoped she would one day return to the ranch, to him. I wondered of his secret dreams for them both. What does he dream of now?

Four days after the final shots had been fired, the three of us sat alone at this skeletal ranch. We warmed ourselves outside, around a morning campfire, no one voicing the idea, the fear that the house itself was a place we did not wish to spend time yet. If ever.

Jack rubbed cold and stiffness from his knees and hands, beginning to look rested, though his beard and buckskins had a long way to go before they resembled their former selves. He caught my eye and looked away. Odd, as he is usually chatty in the morning. Hell, he's usually chatty all the time.

I poured another cup of coffee and looked around at the long, low land, grassed in this special valley. It sits ringed with ample stands of timber that, if treated with respect, would serve to supply Thomas, as the rightful deed holder, with income aplenty. Then there were the water rights from the Snake River, flowing as it did nearly through the center of the ranch proper.

Yes sir, I had to admit the spread was not a bad spot at all, and came with as much potential as any such place could offer. It would need the right foreman, that would be the key to Thomas's success. He was incapable, at least at present, of running anything but his mouth.

But he was a bright young man and I held out hope he would learn all the place required of him. And in turn he would be repaid a hundredfold. The great question mark at the end of the sentence, of course, remained: Would he have the ambition to stick with it?

I sipped and warmed the back of one hand before the fire. Then it came to me, Jack was feeling the urge to light out. I can't say as I blamed him. He could, after all, be trapped there, winter in the mountains being a fickle but certain presence.

As for myself, I wasn't ready to leave yet. I wasn't even certain I wanted to leave. Over the night, a spark of an idea had settled in my mind and refused to wink out. I decided to blow on it to see if it caught flame.

"Thomas," I cleared my throat. "Now that you have this place secured, well, there's a whole lot of potential here, you know. The timber alone, plus the water rights, all this open land." I leaned forward, warming to the topic. "This little valley looks to be particularly fertile, I'd wager that's been so even in drier years than this one has been. I know you don't have much experience in ranching, but with the right foreman . . ." I let the thought trail, and sort of smiled at that point. I know I turned a little red. I can't help it, I always do that whenever I'm tooting my own horn.

"Well, what I'm getting at is, I'd be willing to settle in for a spell, say, through the winter, maybe into spring, help you get the place up and working. I can't say I know all there is to know about ranching, but I've done my bit of riding for a brand. I'd be glad to share what I know."

I leaned forward further, trying to ignore the stone-still silence rolling in waves from Maple Jack. At that moment I didn't much care what Jack thought. This idea of mine was suddenly taking shape. The more I spoke, the more it seemed attainable, full of promise. It felt right, somehow.

Jack grunted to his feet, tossed the last of his coffee to the ground, and set his tin cup on the stump he'd been occupying. He ambled his way slowly down to the barn. I figured he was checking on the animals. It didn't matter much at the time, as I was preoccupied with great plans, perhaps the best I'd ever come up with. And I was eager to discuss them with Thomas, my little brother. Heck, if it all worked out, I might one day share that bit of family history with him.

"Why, I'll bet we could find a decent crew this fall, hire them on with the promise of future earnings. Of course, you'd have to give them a warm bed and three meals a day. There will be plenty of work for them come winter and spring. Beeves to run, timber to harvest." I gestured broadly at the open meadow before us.

I admit I laid it on thick, like fresh butter on a slab of steaming-hot bread. But I had other reasons, too, for dogging this line of thought. I'd begun to like having Thomas around, despite his irritating ways. I liked having a long-lost little brother around.

"I figure you can get a loan on the value of the land, and if you're careful with your spending, you can build up quite a herd here. This valley is promising. Why, look what Scribley did with his place." It was risky to say, given how the man had ended up, all he had done to people, but I have a way of saying things, then wishing I'd kept my yap closed. Always too late.

"Well, what do you say, Thomas? I'm willing to stick around if you are, help you settle in, get the spread righted, hire a crew, see what's what."

Thomas grew quiet, looked down at his feet, then looked up at me again, shaking his head and smiling. There was that tone, that cock to his head. "What grandiose visions! What, really, are you talking about? You don't honestly think I'm going to stay out here do you? I'm going to sell this prime piece of real estate to the highest bidder." The boy looked at me as if I were a tenant farmer on his estate, worrying my hat brim in my calloused hands, afraid to meet his eye.

"I fancy I'll do all right, too," he said, flexing his nostrils and stretching his back. "It's a nicely sited place, from what you've told me. And from what I can gather, it has the all-important good water rights. That apparently means a lot out here. No, sir, I'll be selling up. I figure I'll get the best price by actually being here. Of course I'll need your help in righting the place around. So yes, in so far as your presence is required here, you may stay on, Scorfano. For the time being."

The smug little whelp used that foul name again, and wrapped it in that equally foul air of class distinction. Doing his utmost to put me in my place. Or the place he wanted me, at any rate.

I sat still for a moment. I was too busy clearing the dewy cobwebs from my mind. I had done it once more. I had fallen for his charms, the bald innocence of his using ways. My own gullibility pelted my head like a sudden hailstorm. My foolishness at times knows no bounds.

I stood and tossed the coffee grounds out of my pot, along the edge of the fire. I gathered my belongings, taking my time. It would not have mattered to Thomas, anyway. He was lost in his own rich-boy world, and talking as fast as he was able about how wonderfully cultured the people are back East.

"Just think, Scorfano, I'll finally be able once again to hold my head up. Oh, perhaps not in Washington yet, but maybe in Richmond. I hear it's quite a festive place once more."

Something snapped him from his daydream. He saw me putting my gear together. "Hey, what are you doing, Scorfano?" Thomas grinned. "Or should I say . . . foreman?"

I didn't answer.

"I said, what are you doing?" Thomas crossed his arms, stretched his legs out toward the fire, a slight smile playing at his mouth.

I stopped buckling the saddlebag and looked at him. "I'm leaving."

"You can't do that." His grin slipped a little. "I haven't officially hired you yet. Let alone given you permission to leave."

"The hell I can't."

That is when the truth began to dawn on him. He stood, his hands wringing together like two hairless pink rats wrestling.

229

"Why would you leave?"

"Because, Sir High-and-Mighty, there isn't room enough on this range, despite your vast acreage, for me and you . . . and your ego."

CHAPTER THIRTY-FIVE

Thomas did not understand me.

I shouldered my gear and headed to the barn.

"Where will you go?" he said, trailing after me. His voice sounded small, unsure, and weak once more.

"Anywhere." I thought to myself that Oregon might be worth exploring, head on over to the Pacific. It had been a while. Or maybe I would drift on down to Old Mexico. That, too, had been a while. Not like it mattered. Eventually some fool would think I was some other fool and the whole thing would happen again.

That's the one solid notion about most people, they're predictable. They never let you down. It's the ones that aren't that you have to watch out for. They're the best and worst kind. They keep you guessing, because they catch you unaware and then let you have it. I know Thomas sure did.

By that time, Jack had gathered his small amount of gear and had it cinched atop his packhorse. Oddly enough, my saddle and tack were piled on a rack outside Tiny's stall. I didn't look over at Jack as I saddled my horse and mounted up. He climbed aboard Ol' Mossy and wound his way out of the open barn door.

"But Scorfano, what will I do? Where will I go?"

"I expect you'll be busy enough readying this spread for sale."

"Which way is town? Where is the outhouse?"

I rode out of the barn and up the lane, soon keeping pace to

Jack's right. To his great credit, Jack didn't crack a smile nor make a sound. He had known what would happen between me and Thomas back there at the campfire. And there he'd been in the barn, all but expecting me.

As we rode, our animals' hooves swished through brittle, late-season grasses, sounding light and free like birds' wings.

"Scorfano! Roamer! I'll starve! Help me, Roamer! Help!"

He wouldn't starve. That much I was sure of. I left him a half pound of coffee beans. Hell, that's all a man needs, anyway. Good cup of coffee of a morning, a solid horse under him, a good book or three, a skinning knife, maybe a long gun, and an urge to not care where he's going. Else he might miss something along the way. I'd learned much of that from Maple Jack.

I looked over at my mentor. The old man's stout profile was straight and sure in the saddle, a pleased, relaxed expression on his whiskered face. It was the first sure sign of happiness I'd seen there in a long time. I reckoned I still had a lot to learn.

And so we rode on out, Tiny Boy full of himself and clipping a solid pace, Ol' Mossback matching him, stride for stride, in his silent, steadfast way.

The last sound we heard was the fearful, angry voice of Thomas, my own flesh, and the one person in the world I was most closely related to, by blood anyway.

"I will never forgive you!" shouted Thomas. "I wish . . . I wish I had the strength to shoot you!"

"So do I," I said to myself, as Maple Jack and I rode north. "So do I."

The end.
Roamer and Maple Jack will return. . . .

ABOUT THE AUTHOR

Matthew P. Mayo is an award-winning author of more than twenty-five books and dozens of short stories. His novel, *Tucker's Reckoning,* won the Western Writers of America's Spur Award for Best Western Novel, and his short stories have been Spur Award and Peacemaker Award finalists. His many novels include *Winters' War; Wrong Town; Hot Lead, Cold Heart; The Hunted; Shotgun Charlie;* and others.

Matthew's numerous nonfiction books include the bestselling *Cowboys, Mountain Men & Grizzly Bears; Haunted Old West; Jerks in New England History;* and *Hornswogglers, Fourflushers & Snake-Oil Salesmen.* He has been an on-screen expert for a popular BBC-TV series about lost treasure in the American West, and has had three books optioned for film.

Matthew and his wife, photographer Jennifer Smith-Mayo, run Gritty Press (www.GrittyPress.com) and rove the byways of North America in search of hot coffee, tasty whiskey, and high adventure. For more information, drop by Matthew's Web site at www.MatthewMayo.com.